A JIGGY'S GENES STORY

JIGGY'S
MAGIC
BALLS

MICHAEL LAWRENCE

ORCHARD BOOKS

ORCHARD BOOKS
338 Euston Road, London NW1 3BH
Orchard Books Australia
Level 17/207 Kent Street, Sydney, NSW 2000

First published in the UK in 2010

ISBN 978 1 40830 803 5

3 5 7 9 10 8 6 4 2

Orchard Books is a division of Hachette Children's Books,
an Hachette UK company.

www.hachette.co.uk

JiGGY'S MAGiC BALLS

Don't miss the original Jiggy McCue series!

Visit Michael Lawrence's website:
www.wordybug.com

And find loads of Jiggy fun at:
www.jiggymccue.co.uk

*'The gene that didn't look after its own
interests would not survive.'*
Richard Dawkins

Now get this. I'm out with my mum buying underpants *yet again*! Neither of us ever learns when it comes to my underpants. She never learns not to drag me along, and I never learn to scream loud enough to bust her eardrums.

'Mother,' I say, far too calmly, 'I do not – repeat, not – need a constant supply of new pants. Remember your washing machine? What you do is, you open the door every month or so and pop my latest pair in, and next time you open it they're as good as new. We do not – repeat again, do *not* – have to buy more pants every Saturday of my life.'

'It's your birthday in a couple of weeks, Jiggy,' she replied.

'Yes – so?'

'You must have new pants for your birthday.'

'Why, you're not gonna make me strip down to them to blow my candles out, are you?'

But she'd stopped listening. She does that a lot, my mother. Switches off when I utter words. I might as well not be there half the time. A life-size Jiggy doll could stand in for me. It could just be sat in a chair, or slotted onto rollerblades to go shopping with her, and it would never answer back or express a personal opinion. She'd like that.

Towards the end of this pathetic excuse for a conversation we'd walked past the window of a shop in Britney Spears Arcade. I strolled on for a while until I realised I was alone. Then I considered making a break for it while I could, but (because I'm a good, kind, caring son) returned to the window to see if the old dear was still in this world or leaning against the glass because her spleen or whatever had packed up.

'Mum,' I said. 'I have a life. Well, sort of. A life I don't want to waste hour after hour of while you look in every window we pass on the way to the Oxfam pant shop.'

'Look at this,' she said, like I once again hadn't spoken.

I looked in the shop window.

'Terrific. Can we go now?'

'No, look at this.'

I looked again, because I'm the good, kind, blah-blah son mentioned above. There wasn't much in the window, just a big notice on an easel and a big shield like people used in olden times when riding horses and smiting one another with swords and stuff. I quite liked the look of the shield. It was red, with a black lion on it.

'Cool,' I said.

'D'you think so?' said Mum.

'Mm.' It sounded like it was what she wanted to hear.

'You're not just saying that?'

'Well, yes, I am just saying it. That's because I just said it. Now let's be on our way, shall we? Urgent pants to buy before the weekend closes and I head schoolward with a heavy sigh yet again.'

'But it does appeal to you?' she said as we walked away.

I slapped my forehead. 'It appeals to me. You want it written in blood? If so, let's use yours.'

'I was just thinking that it would make an unusual birthday present.'

9

'For me?' I said.

'Of course for you. Would you like it?'

'Well...yeah. I guess.'

I didn't know what use a shield would be, couldn't see myself carrying it on my arm around the estate, but I supposed it would look pretty fair on my bedroom wall. And a shield had to be better than most of the junk the Golden Oldies offload on me once a year – twice if you count Christmas.

My birthday eventually arrived, and for a change it wasn't a school day. I would have stayed in bed longer for that very reason, but my mother likes to hoick me out of my pit by the hair around dawn on birthday morns because she can't wait to give me the latest piece of rubbish she's wasted the housekeeping on. I knew what to expect this time, though, so I put on my best Hey-can't-wait-to-get-at-that-shield face for her benefit. The adult male in our house plays hardly any part in present-giving. Mum shops for all the pressies except her own (but sometimes for those too) and wraps them up and writes the sweet little kissy-kissy labels, and Dad stands around smiling in a faintly embarrassed nothing-to-do-with-me sort of way while the traditional giving/receiving/unwrapping/joyful-expression process occurs.

Because I was expecting a big lion-covered shield, the A4 envelope Mum handed over was a bit on the puzzling side. 'Looked bigger in the window,' I said.

'That was just to draw people in,' Mum said. 'This is more detailed.'

'More detailed?'

'Open it.'

I noticed a word in the top left-hand corner of the envelope.

'So that's what you think of me,' I said.

'What do you mean?' said Mum.

I showed her the word. GIT.

She laughed. 'No, no, that's the firm that does all this.'

'All what?'

'Open the envelope and you'll see.'

There was a white folder in the envelope, and inside the folder a few sheets of printed paper.

'What's this? An invitation from the shop to go pick it up in person?'

'Pick what up in person?' Mum said brightly.

'The shield, what else?'

Her brightness dimmed a tad. 'Shield?'

'Just read it and get it over with, Jig,' said Dad wearily.

'Read it?' I said. 'Father. Birthdays are for putting the birthday feet up and being waited on by doting parents, not reading – 'cept comics and annuals maybe.'

But I pasted the McCue eyeballs to the top sheet of paper like the dutiful son I was trying so hard to be because this was a Special Day. Here's what was printed on the sheet.

Think you're unique? Think again! The very latest genealogical research shows that each of us shares entire swathes of genes with some of our ancestors, which means that you're not the first to have those eyes, that hair, that attitude. Now GIT can track your genetic fingerprints back through the years and reveal the person you could have been in a previous age!

'What does GIT stand for?' I asked.

'Genetic Investigations in Time,' said Mum.

'And "reveal the person you could have been in a previous age" means...?'

'It's explained in more detail in the documentation, but I asked the people in the shop to talk me through it so we'd know what we were paying for. They told me that science is now able to identify ancestors who share one's DNA almost to the last freckle, and all it takes is a little saliva.'

'Saliva? Whose?'

'In this case, yours. Be little point in giving them a sample of a neighbour's to identify your ancestors, would there?'

'So I have to go to the shop and hurl into something?'

'No, no, all they needed was a swab, and they had that ten days ago. Their first results should be in this folder.'

'I haven't given anyone a swab of saliva.'

'No. I did. I took it one night when you were asleep with your mouth open.'

My mouth fell open again, but not to give spit. 'Are you telling me that you snuck into my room

13

and took the juice of my gob without *permission*?'

'I had to, or this wouldn't have been such a surprise.'

'Surprise or no surprise, it's a bit of a liberty.'

'But worth it, I'm sure. The GIT computers immediately started tracking back through the years trying to pinpoint similar DNA patterns to yours. You have thousands of ancestors, of course, and share genes with all of them, but only a select few will have had precisely the same arrangement as you.'

'You're not telling me they were *exactly* like me,' I said uneasily.

'According to GIT,' said Mum, 'they would have been as like you as identical twins, in looks, personality, the way they approached situations, virtually everything.'

'Gawd 'elp us,' Dad muttered from the sidelines. 'Other Jiggys all through history. Doesn't bear thinking about.'

'At least they're unlikely to be football fanatics like this one's father,' Mum said sharply.

'Speaking of which, I'd better get ready,' he said. 'They're kicking off early today. One of my team's getting married on the pitch afterwards to the last winner of *Anyone With Big Boobs Can Sing*.'

'Mel, it's your son's birthday. Football can wait.'

He gasped. 'Football can *wait*? Oh, if only other members of my family shared my planet! Happy birthday, Jig.'

'Let me get this straight,' I said to my mother while Dad went to fetch his scarf and rattle. 'These GITs are searching the past for reverse clones of me? Of *me*?'

'That's the idea,' she said. 'The science isn't yet sufficiently advanced for them to identify Jiggy types in chronological order, they say, but they guarantee to locate one a month from some point in history for the duration of our direct debit payments.'

'And how long's that?'

'We've signed their minimum contract for three monthly payments, but if the results are satisfactory we can extend them until they can find no more Jiggys.'

Other Jiggys before me? I wasn't sure I liked the sound of that. I'd always thought of myself as a total original. Mum must have noticed that I'd started to tap my feet and flap my elbows, the way I do when I'm on edge, because her happy smile got a bit crimped round the edges.

'You read the ad in the window telling us all about it,' she said. 'You seemed keen at the time.'

'I was looking at the shield,' I explained. 'Thought you were too.'

Her jaw sagged like an empty jockstrap.

'The shield? Not the big notice announcing research that can identify other versions of a person?'

She sounded so close to distress that she'd got it wrong that Good, Kind, Caring Jiggy tore off his shirt and bared his mighty Superkid of the Day chest.

'Only kidding,' the soft nit chirruped moronically. 'The shield was cool, but this is what I really wanted. Didn't think I'd get it, is all.'

The aged parent's face brightened. 'Really?'

'Really. Fantastic. Wow. What a birthday present.'

She looked relieved as she rummaged through the folder. 'Let's see who the computers have found among your ancestors for our first payment, shall we?'

She started reading another sheet of paper – silently, to herself, like I wasn't in the room. As she read, her eyes widened.

'Yes?' I said.

'They've found someone who matches your genetic pattern in the 15th century!'

I goggled. 'The 15th? Someone like me in the 15th century? Is there a photo?'

She looked up. 'A photo? Of a 15th-century Jiggy?'

'All right then, what did he do?'

She read some more, just as silently. 'Golly,' she said.

'Golly what?'

'He seems to have been attached to some noble knight.'

'Knight? As in armour?'

'Seems so, yes. Isn't that something?'

She handed over the paper. It was made up to look like an ancient scroll, with olde-worlde writing and all. I read it, all the way to the bottom, even though it was my birthday. There was a lot of waffle but next to nothing about what this 15th-century version of me did, only that he probably looked like me. Guess you were expected to fill in the gaps with your imagination. Bit of a cop-out, I thought, though I didn't say so out loud. I also didn't say that I had better ways of wasting my time than wondering about a person who lived six centuries before my own. He could tell his own story.

Or keep it to himself. Up to him.

JiGGY'S MAGiC BALLS

AS TOLD BY THE 15TH-CENTURY JiGGY

Well, here I am, up to my armpits in mud and rust, talking to myself once again. I talk to myself because mine are the only ears that listen to me. No one else's listen because I'm just another peasant kid. I'm not even a squire yet, even if I do serve a knight with a full suit of armour. My knight is Sir Bozo de Beurk, and his armour isn't much better than scrap metal, but that's not the point. A knight's a knight and armour's armour if you close your eyes. Sir Bozo isn't the brightest light in the knight sky, but at least his wife isn't about any more. His wife was called Ratface. Well, that's what I called her. Lady Ratface thought she was really something. Always trying to make out that her origins weren't almost as humble as mine. 'Ow! So-nace-to-mate-yer,' she'd coo when she was introduced to people she wanted to impress. Didn't impress me one bit. Not that she tried. Just shouted orders at me the whole time and called me names. I wasn't fond of her.

As well as a wife, Sir Bozo had a castle once. Crumbling old place, very draughty, left to him by some distant cousin who'd run out of other surviving relatives. Rubbish as it was, Bozo was quite fond of the castle, probably because he'd never had one of his own before. When Lady Ratface decided she could do better than Bozo in the knight department she hired this dodgy legal wizard, Spivvel Merlin, who had a rep for getting good deals for greedy wives. Sir Bozo wasn't hugely rich, though, so all Merlin got for Lady R was the lousy castle, which she immediately put up for sale. There were no takers, but then Merlin himself made an offer for it, and she accepted, so it was his now, which really choked Sir B because him and Merlin had been mortal enemies since they were at school together.

After the divorce, the only possessions Sir Bozo was left with were his horse, a shed on boggy ground, an allotment, and an old sword he won at school way back. The boggy shed was where we lived and the allotment was where most of our food came from. Sometimes he sent me to the nearby river to catch fish. I wasn't great at that, so fish was off the menu more often than on it. Because he missed castle life, Sir Bozo spent the last of his loot on wooden battlements for the shed and a drawbridge for the moat we didn't have. He tried to get a moat going by peeing from the battlements, and gave me instructions to do likewise. The flies were quite thick round Castle-de-Beurk-on-the-Allotment.

There wasn't a whole lot to do once I'd performed my menial duties, so it was just as well I had a hobby. I carved things out of wood. Things like back-scratchers, animals, spoons, stuff like that. The day the big something happened that was to change my life I was sitting on the drawbridge (a plank) over the piddling moat putting the finishing touches to an egg.

'You have quite a gift,' a smooth voice said.

I looked up. Spiv Merlin. I'd only seen him once before, but I'd know him anywhere because he wasn't like anyone else. He was very tall, with ultra-black hair (dyed) and a long droopy moustache, kind of oily-looking, that he was always stroking. There was a sweet smell about him, like overripe apples.

'Yours for a small fee,' I replied. 'Or a large one if you're feeling generous.'

He smirked. 'What would I do with a wooden egg? Eat it with wooden teeth?'

'It's an ornament. It's to go in the wooden egg cup I'm making next.'

'Really. Well, one thing I don't need is cheap ornaments.'

'Ornaments are only cheap if you don't pay much for them,' I said.

'They're even cheaper if you don't pay anything,' he chuckled, and quit the scene in a hurry. He'd noticed Sir Bozo heading our way.

'What was that creep doing here?' Sir B wanted to know when he joined me.

'Wasting my time,' I said, polishing my egg with a cloth.

'Sire,' he said.

'Eh?' I said.

'You're supposed to call me sire because I'm your lord and master. I don't know how many times I've told you that.'

'Me neither. Lost count after time twenty-three.'

23

'Have you pulled the cabbages for lunch?'

'No.'

'Sire.'

'You're welcome.'

'Why haven't you pulled the cabbages like I told you to?'

'Because they're full of slugs.'

'Slugs? There are slugs in the cabbages?'

'Yes.'

'There are slugs in the cabbages and you left them there?'

'Yes.'

'Why?'

'They looked so happy.'

'You useless little peasant!' he cried, swiping me round the head. 'I can't remember the last time I had roast slug!'

And he rushed to the cabbage patch and started tearing up cabbages by the fistful. I rubbed my head and sighed. It was going to be roast slug six meals in a row. Just as I was getting used to being a vegetarian.

CHAPTER TWO

I don't usually dance in the same circles as bigwigs like Spivvel Merlin, so I was surprised when he approached me again the next day. Like before, I was sitting on the drawbridge, but this time I was oiling Sir Bozo's armour, trying to make it look better than it was for the tournament he was jousting in tomorrow and the day after.

'Is he about?' Merlin asked.

'If you mean Sir B, no.'

'Good. Got a spot of business for you.'

I squinted up at him. 'Business? For me?'

'Yes. I want you to carve me a pair of wooden balls.'

You might not be surprised to hear that a minute's silence followed this.

'Well?' he said at last.

'Well what?'

'Have you nothing to say?'

'I've got lots to say, but they're all jokes you might not like.'

He dipped into a leather bag and took out two brightly coloured balls. Different colours on each one, swirly sort of pattern.

'Can you copy these?'

I examined the balls in his hand. 'Tricky,' I said.

'Why? You had no trouble carving that egg yesterday.'

'That was an egg. How perfect do you want the copies?'

'I want them exactly like these – I mean *exactly* – and in a hurry.'

'Sorry then, no can do. Perfection takes time.'

'You have till just after lunch tomorrow.'

'I'd need longer.'

'You can't have longer. I have to give these to my cl—' He stopped. Started half of that again. '...to my sister tomorrow afternoon. They were our father's, you see. He left them to her in his will.'

'Your father left his balls to your sister?'

'When he died.'

'Best time,' I said.

'I'd pay you.'

My eyes probably flared at this. The only money they usually saw was other people's. Sir Bozo paid me nothing. All I got from him in return for my services was a heap of straw to sleep on, and he said I should be grateful for that.

'How much?' I asked Merlin.

He stroked his long black moustache. 'I'll give you half a groat. For the pair.'

I shook my bonce. 'Half a groat per ball or no deal.'

He snarled. Like most rich people he didn't like parting with money. 'Very well. But the paintwork better be good.'

'You want them painted too?'

'Of course I want them painted. If they're not they won't look like these, will they? You can paint, can't you?'

'Sure I can. I paint rats sometimes.'

'Rats?'

'Carved ones. I like to do them in bright colours.'

'You're a pretty weird kid, aren't you?' he said.

'You're a pretty weird legal wizard,' I answered.

'Less of the lip, boy. Can you paint my balls or not?'

'I suppose. Long as Sir Bozo doesn't suddenly find extra jobs for me.'

'Where is old Bozo anyway?' he asked.

'He's helping put the tourney tents up in return for pigeon soup and lumpy bread.'

Merlin laughed. 'The great Sir Bozo de Beurk putting up tents! How the mighty are fallen.'

'He's better off than me,' I said. 'He gets soup and bread, I get the burnt remains of last night's slug fritters.'

'So it's agreed then,' Merlin said.

'What is?'

'That you'll have a pair of balls exactly like these ready for me to collect by just after lunch tomorrow.'

'I'll give it a go.'

'Painted and dry,' he added.

'They will be.'

'If they're not perfect I won't pay you.'

'They'll be perfect.' I really wanted that groat.

Merlin handed me his balls. 'Guard them with your life and show them to no one. I'll be back just before two o'clock tomorrow.'

And he went.

I found a small block of wood and put the

painted balls on the ground between my legs to copy them (balls, not legs). I'd just started work when I saw Sir Bozo coming back. I slammed my legs shut so he wouldn't see his enemy's balls and oiled some more armour. Sir B wasn't in a great mood, but that was nothing new. Ever since his wife got his castle he'd been going on and on and on about how hard-done-by he was.

'Here am I,' he muttered as he stepped onto the plank (I mean drawbridge), 'a knight who's fought battle after battle, rescued damsel after damsel—'

'One damsel,' I said. 'From a hedge. She was drunk.'

'—and I'm putting up tents for soup and bread, like some nobody.'

'Yeah, Spiv Merlin thought that was pretty funny too.'

I said this to myself, but he heard. His wits might not be too sharp, but he has the ears of a bat (they stick out).

'Merlin?' he said. 'He's been here again?'

'He wandered by.' I'd already said it, so I couldn't deny it.

'He wandered by and you told him I was putting up tents?'

'Yes, well, you know how these things slip out.'

He slapped me round the head.

'Stupid boy! Have you no loyalty?'

'I might have if you didn't do that every time I did something you didn't like.'

'That man,' he growled. 'Have you heard what he's done now?'

'Not yet,' I said, stroking my head. 'But I bet every last carrot on the allotment that I'm about to.'

'I'll tell you what he's done. He sued this wandering magician for not performing real magic like it said on the poster.'

'The carrots are mine!' I cried.

'The magician's been banished from the county, but before he went he was ordered to hand over all his props, so now he's just another strolling peasant, as if there weren't enough of those already. I hate that man!'

'The magician?'

'*Merlin*, you ragged urchin!'

And he stormed off, but not before landing another head smack. As he went I grabbed Merlin's balls and banged them together, wishing Bozo's head was between them. 'Ragged urchin yourself,' I said, turning away to spit. But then I heard a shout and looked back. Right where Sir Bozo had been stood a boy of about my age, in clothes even dirtier and more wrinkled than mine. The shout hadn't come from him, though, but from a pasty-faced weasel-eyed man on a dusty carthorse who'd yelled at him for not jumping out of the way as he clopped up.

It was nothing to do with me and I should have just minded my own business, but I was still annoyed at being so badly treated by Sir B, so I took the little block of wood I'd started work on and tossed it under the carthorse's hooves. This caused the horse to stumble and its rider to fly over its neck and land face down on the drawbridge in front of me.

'Hey, good bird impression,' I said.

He hadn't seen me toss the wood, but I wasn't surprised when he jumped up and slapped me round the head.

'Cheeky bumpkin,' he snarled.

Then he got back in the saddle, whipped the

horse's flanks like it was all its fault, and rode on.

Three head slaps in two minutes. It's no fun being a peasant kid in this day and age. No fun at all.

CHAPTER THREE

Because I'm only a peasant I don't get a bed, but as our floor's so damp (water bubbles up here and there from time to time) I'd built myself one out of wood. The straw on top was definitely better than nothing, but it was still a pretty hard bed, so I often had trouble dropping off.* That night was one of those times, and I'd only just managed it when the door crashed back and Sir B stumbled in. The moon was beaming through a crack in the wall, so I could see that he didn't look himself, which had to be a good thing. Sir Bozo wasn't like his old rival Merlin in any way except age. While Merlin was long and lean, Bozo was kind of squat – not short exactly, not fat exactly, but chunky. Also unlike Merlin, he didn't dye his hair or have a droopy moustache, though he had a constant stubble. To tell you the truth, he wasn't much more of a joy to behold than he was to be with.

---

* To sleep, not the bed.

'Dirty stop-out,' I mumbled from my humble wooden bed.

'Dirty stop-out, *sire*,' he replied.

'You look even more dazed than usual.'

'I just woke up.'

'Makes two of us.'

'In a ditch.'

'Makes one of us. What were you doing in a ditch?'

'Dreaming.'

'You don't have to get into a ditch to dream,' I said. 'You can do that in bed. Maybe your mum never told you that.'

'I dreamt I was a ragged urchin, and a man on a horse shouted at me, and I wandered off and got a kicking from the people putting up the tents because they wouldn't believe I was who I said I was, and when I got a bit shirty they called these knights over, and they took me round the back of the booze tent and slapped me around a bit, and next thing I knew I woke up in the ditch.'

'Just as well it was only a dream,' I said.

'Only a dream, *sire*.'

'Couldn't have put it better myself.'

He tottered to his big *soft* bed and grabbed the old school sword he kept beside it. Then he settled down with the sword on his chest like he was on his knightly tomb. He'd been sleeping like that ever since he lost his castle. Sad.

Day One of the tournament. It had rained in the night after the moon got sick of shining, but people had still trundled in from miles around to squelch about in the mud and cheer knights clashing and tumbling in the lists. They didn't only come for the jousting, though. There were entertainers – jugglers, clowns, stilt-walkers, fire-eaters – and the dwarf-hurling shy was already doing good business. The stalls heaped with bread and stinky cheeses and stuff were doing well too, and one, selling a weird foreign dish called peetsa, was practically under siege. There were also a few runny-nosed merchants selling wooden squirrels, mice and birds, which made me wish I'd thought to carve some myself. Too late now, but at least I'd got the copies of Merlin's balls done in time. I was pleased with what I'd done. My balls looked so much like Merlin's that no one could have told them apart. No one who didn't have eyes as good as mine, that is, because the one thing I hadn't copied was the two little words tucked away in the swirling colour of the originals. The word on one ball was 'Devils'. The word on the other was 'Little'.

Unfortunately, mine and Merlin's weren't the only balls around. A shouty game was going on in the field next to the tourney ground. They call it foot-ball, but most of the footwork occurs when a player kicks anyone who gets in his way while he's running with the ball in his arms. The ball is an inflated pig's bladder and the only rule seems to be to get it from one end of the field to the other. Anyone can join in a foot-ball match and sometimes there's a lot more people on one side than the other, and because some players carry shields and weapons it can turn into a bit of a massacre. There was this town mayor once who issued a decree banning the game because it was so dangerous and disturbed the peace. Anyone caught playing it would be chucked in the chokey, the mayor said, but this only happened once.* The chokey was stormed and the jailor's head lopped

---

* The chokey = prison.

off and used as a ball in the next match. The mayor kept his trap shut about foot-ball after that.

When Merlin turned up just before two I held out the two pairs of painted balls and told him to spot the diff.

'No problem,' he said, snatching one of the pairs.

'Wrong,' I said.

He gave me a disbelieving sneer and looked towards the foot-ball field where maniacs were still beating one another up over the pig's bladder. Then he banged the balls together and muttered something.

'Why'd you do that?' I asked.

'Wait,' he said.

'What for?'

'Just wait.'

We waited. Nothing happened. He turned back to me.

'Give me the other pair.'

I gave him the other pair and he faced the unbeautiful game once more. Then he banged the balls together, muttered, and four of the players leapt into the air, did double somersaults, and came down on one another's shoulders. That is, three of them came down on one another's shoulders. The fourth didn't have any shoulders to stand on because his feet were on the ground and the others were on top of him in a teetering tower. A few heartbeats later he collapsed under them.

Merlin turned back to me. He was smiling now, but it wasn't one of those great-job-you-did-there sort of smiles. Not a bit of it.

'Thought you could fool me, did you, boy?'

'I wasn't trying to fool you. I told you they were the real ones and you didn't believe me. Er...those balls didn't make the footie nuts do that, did they?'

'They did, yes.'

'How?'

He didn't answer right away, like he was thinking, 'Should I tell him?' But then he decided. 'Well, I suppose there's no harm in your knowing. These belonged to a magician I sued for a client and they're now my client's property. I'm meeting him shortly to hand them over.'

'So they weren't your dad's and you're not meeting your sister.'

'I've cut my dad out of my will and I don't have a sister.'

'And they can make people do stuff?'

'They can do various things.'

'How do they work?'

'You bang them together while saying what you want to happen,' he said, 'and it happens.'

'You mean if you banged them while saying something like, say, "Become a ragged urchin" to some knight he would...?'

'Become a ragged urchin, yes.'

'Wow. Balls like that could make a person's fortune.'

'Only if he was really clever,' said Merlin.

'How's that?'

'According to the previous owner (I slipped him a couple of groats for telling me this before they frogmarched him out of the county) the balls can't do anything for the user. But a sharp operator could use them to make someone else prosper and do quite nicely out of the deal.'

'Take a cut of the profits, you mean?'

'Something like that.'

'But why did you want copies of the balls if you have to give them to your client? There's no magic in the copies.'

'Mementoes,' he said, popping the magic balls into a secret pocket inside his cloak and my copies into the bag he'd taken the real ones out of yesterday.

'Mind you don't get them mixed up,' I said.

'No fear of that.' He glanced at a bracelet on his wrist. 'I must go. My client will be waiting.'

I held my hand out. 'One groat please.'

He shook his head. 'I don't pay for shoddy workmanship.'

I frowned. 'Shoddy? You couldn't tell mine from the real ones.'

He sneered. 'Of course I could. And I'm not satisfied. In future I'll take my balls elsewhere.'

I could only gape after him as he walked away with a sprightly spring in his step. All that brilliant work for nothing!

CHAPTER FOUR

Billy Camlot's Travelling Tourneys

These were the words on the droopy banner at the entrance to the tournament ground. It was all pretty seedy-looking. There were loads of flags, but they were grubby, with ragged ends that jerked in the breeze, and there were signs that screamed BEWARE OF PICKPOCKETS. They'll be disappointed if they pick *my* pocket, I thought.

When he takes part in a joust I have to help Sir B into his armour. I buckle his straps, force his feet into boots that are too small for him, jam his helmet on his fat head, and give him a lift up onto Saggy, his horse. Saggy's full name is Sagramor. I call him Saggy because he droops in the middle when Sir B gets on him in full armour. The man's no shrimp at the best of times, but add his armour to his weight and it's a wonder the poor old nag can go two steps without dropping to his knees. Sir B's present suit is heavier than his old one, which was one of the few other things Merlin got for Lady Ratface in the divorce settlement. The cheapo suit the big B clanks around in now was bought from a third-hand armour dealer called d'Grott. It's made of very inferior metal. Starts to rust if a cloud appears in the sky.

Sir Bozo was having one of his tourneys-aren't-like-they-used-to-be grumbles as I led him to the lists (on Saggy) for his first joust of the weekend.

'You don't see many really decent knights in these events since the health and safety bods made us put blunts on our lances,' he said. 'Risk was what made these things worth attending. There's more risk in picking wild roses than tilting a lance today. And they let any old riffraff in. Hard to believe that jousting was once the sport of gentlemen.'

'Sport of berks, you mean,' I muttered.

His fat metal chest swelled with pride. 'Indeed it was, lad. My father, Sir Twitter de Beurk, and my grandfather, Sir Crétin de Beurk, were both committed jousters.'

'Committed,' I said. 'Yeah, I bet.'

He nodded. 'Great knights, both of them.'

'What happened to them?'

His eyes slid sideways. 'They died.'

'How?'

'Jousting.'

His first opponent was Sir Wilfred d'Retch of Little-Haven-in-the Crotch. Sir Wilfred's armour was fresh out of the box, and so was he. I saw his face just before his squire popped his helmet on. He was about a third Sir Bozo's age, and he looked like he'd rather be anywhere than on a horse with a lance in his fist racing towards another lance, even if it did have a blunt end.

I got Saggy into position at our end of the lists and climbed the steps that were placed there for the helper to put his knight's helmet on for him. I was just fitting Sir B's helmet when he started whining about probably being the only knight there without a squire.

'You can't afford a squire,' I reminded him. 'You can only just afford me, and that's because you don't pay me anything.'

I slammed his visor shut and was halfway down

the steps when I heard a rumble inside his helmet. I went back up. Lifted his visor.

'Wossup?'

'I forgot to have a pee.'

'Well, save it for the moat. Pee in this crummy armour and it'll rust all down the legs in a second and everyone will know.'

'Everyone will know, *sire*.'

I shut his visor again and jumped off the steps just as the trumpet went. They always give a trumpet blast at jousts if they can find one. When they can't, they bang a drum. When they can't drum up a drum they get someone with a loud voice to shout something like 'Next pair of armoured meatheads *now* please!'. Then a herald comes on and announces the combatants, and the combatants charge one another (on horseback) and try and score a hit with their lances, and if the audience is in luck one of the knights falls off and breaks something. The amount of points a knight can earn depends on how well he strikes his opponent in the opinion of the judges. The knight with the most points at the end of our two-day tourney would be awarded a trophy and a pot of cash – not the huge prize you see at better events, but Sir B needed whatever he could get. Unfortunately, he got off to a bad start when his opponent's horse skidded at the first charge and Sir Wilfred flew back over his saddle and hit the ground with the dull *chwhump* of metal in mud. Sir Bozo was the winner all right, but because he hadn't actually struck Sir Wilf he was only awarded one point, which was one point next to nothing.

'Hardly worth getting out of bed for,' he growled as Saggy wheezed back to our end.

'You're lucky to have a bed to not get out of,' I said.

'You know what this means, don't you?'

'Yes, it means you'll never get enough points to scoop the big prize now.'

'It means I'll never get enough points to scoop the big prize now.'

'You should have taken my advice and signed up for more than two jousts a day. But you never listen to me.'

'I should have signed up for more than two jousts a day,' he said, proving my point without denting a single brain cell.

His second joust wasn't for a while yet, so when he clanked over to the Gents' Pee Tree (separated by a canvas wall from the Ladies' Pee Pit) Saggy and I went in search of a horse trough. We found one and Saggy was slurping away when we were joined by Sir Wilfred d'Retch's squire and horse. The horse introduced himself to Saggy at the trough and the squire introduced himself to me.

'Ryan de Bryan,' he said.

'Jiggy d'Cuer,' said I.

'Your knight looks pretty experienced.'

'That's because he's pretty old.'

'That was mine's second joust ever. You could tell, couldn't you?'

'I did wonder.'

'His first opened the show. I think they gave him the opening slot to kick things off with a laugh.' He patted his horse's neck. 'He slid off Percival here when his opponent's lance came within a sigh of his shield.'

'It probably takes practice to get the hang of it,' I said generously.

'Sir Wilfred doesn't want to get the hang of it. He's only here because Sir Ector (his old man) thinks a few jousts'll make a man of him. I know for a fact that he'd rather be sitting in front of a mirror writing love poetry. You're so lucky, serving a proper knight.'

'Yeah, lucky, that's me. Some days I have to pinch myself to see if I'm awake. Been a squire long?'

'About twenty-four hours.'

'What were you doing before?'

'I was a poacher's assistant.'

'Oh yes, what did you poach?'

'Eggs and fish, mostly.' He glanced towards the field where sporty lunes were still running about with the pig's bladder. 'Now that's what I'd really like to be doing,' he said wistfully.

'Playing foot-ball?' I said in amazement. He'd seemed quite intelligent till now.

'You bet. If it was possible to make a living at it, they'd have to blow the torches out to get me off the field.'

There wasn't much to say after that, so we went our separate ways.

CHAPTER FIVE

The separate way Saggy and I went took us between the long trousers of a bow-legged man on stilts, round a geezer in a turban lying on a bed of nails, and past a giant of a man standing with his arms folded beside a row of old carts and a notice that said:

Huge Ackman
Used Cart Salesman

Most of the people we thronged with looked happier to be there than I was, but one of those who didn't look so thrilled was a tubby little man I saw chatting to Spiv Merlin. He had to be the client he'd been going to meet, because Merlin had just opened the magician's ball bag to show him what was inside. I steered Saggy behind a tree to eavesdrop.

'Here they are, My Lord, the last of his props,' Merlin said. 'They're not magic, of course, any more than the rest of his gear was.'

The client took the coloured balls out of the bag. 'They seemed magical enough when he used them.'

'Of course they did. That was part of the con. That's why we sued him, for being a fake.'

'I know why we sued him,' the client barked. 'But I thought these things might have some power if nothing else did.'

'He was very convincing,' said Merlin, 'but sadly, they're just bits of painted wood.'

'How do you know?'

'I tested them on your behalf when he finally handed them over. He really wasn't keen on parting with them, but he had no choice.'

'Tested them how?'

'By doing as he did: banging them together while telling them what I wanted them to do.'

'And?'

'Nothing.'

'Well, if it's all the same to you, I'll test them myself.'

'By all means, My Lord.'

The client banged the balls together, and as he banged them he stared at the ground and said: 'Grass – turn pink!'

The grass stayed the same old greeny-brown. This wasn't surprising as the actual magic balls were still in the secret pocket inside Merlin's cloak. So that's why you wanted copies, you crook, I thought. He was even more of a slimeball than I'd imagined.

Saggy and I strolled on, and in a minute we saw someone else I'd had a run-in with recently. The pasty-faced geezer with the weasel eyes who called me a cheeky bumpkin. He was going into a tent with faded blue and green stripes. The board outside the tent told the world who ran it and what her business was.

Mental Meg's Marquee!
Let me show you the way to a better life!
Only one groat! Queue here!

I could have done with a pointer to a better life myself, but I didn't join the queue, partly because there wasn't one and partly because I was seriously groatless thanks to Spiv Merlin. I was curious to see what a really mental person did though, so I climbed on Saggy's back and peeked through a high gap in the closed flaps. The nasty geezer was just getting onto a couch while Mental Meg, all big earrings and cleavage, pulled up a stool and started talking to him like she was his mum asking after his health.

'And how are you today, dear?'

'Terrific, *dear*,' the nasty geezer said. 'How long's this take?'

Mental Meg smiled. 'It depends. What should I call you?'

'Call me?'

'Your name.'

He narrowed his eyes suspiciously. 'What do you want my name for?'

'Well, I think it's so much friendlier when we know who we're talking to,' she answered. 'I'm Meg, for instance.'

'I know who you are, it's on the board outside. But if you must know my name it's Arthur. Arthur Penn.'

'Is that Sir Arthur?'

Wrong question. He curled his lip.

'No, it's not *Sir* Arthur. There's only one *Sir* in my family and that's my brother Sean, damn his eyes.'

'Damn his eyes? Why?'

'Why? Because he got knighted for nothing, that's why – unless you count giving a cup of water to King Oscar of Tinkletown when he said he was a bit dry. Things always fall into Sean's lap. Me, I spend my days riding round looking for the one big break that isn't my neck, and what do I get? Absolute perishing zero, that's what.'

'Oh dear, we don't seem to be a very happy bunny, do we?' said Mental Meg.

Arthur Penn's scowl looked like it would break his head in two. 'I'm no poxy bunny, madam. I'm a man without a future. That's why I stepped in here and coughed up that hard-won groat. Now give me the better life you promised, I haven't got all day.'

'I can't *give* you a better life,' said MM gently. 'I can only point the way to one based on your aura and our conversation.'

'My aura? I haven't got an aura.'

'Everyone's got an aura, dear.'

'Oh. Well check it out then, so we can move this along.'

Meg closed her eyes, sat perfectly still, and stayed that way – until Arthur Penn couldn't bear it any longer.

'I didn't pay to watch you dozing,' he said.

Meg opened one eye. 'Once I've absorbed your aura I should be able to gauge the kind of life-path you should be on. Bear with me please.'

She reclosed her eye and Arthur clamped his lips and twiddled his thumbs while she went on absorbing his manky aura.

At last Meg opened both of her eyes.

'You're a very conflicted person, aren't you?' she said.

'Conflicted?'

'You don't know what to do with your life.'

'You don't have to be a fortune-teller to know that, mainly because I already mentioned it.'

She frowned. 'I'm not a fortune-teller, I'm a mental therapist.'

'And I'm in a hurry,' snapped Arthur. 'Come on, let's have it.'

'Have it?'

'Whatever it is you've got for me.'

'Very well,' said Meg. 'My first suggestion for a life-path to consider...' She paused, like she was thinking how to put it.

'The suspense is killing me,' said Arthur.

'Have you ever considered a caring profession?'

'A what?'

'Looking after people worse off than yourself.'

'I don't know nobody worse off than me.'

'Really?' said Meg. 'But you have your health, don't you?'

He shrugged. 'I s'pose.'

'And you eat regularly?'

'I get by.'

'Well, there are lots of folk who have little to eat and are in very poor health, which makes them much worse off than you.'

'I don't care,' said Arthur.

'You don't care? At all?'

'Nope. So maybe that's not the job for me. Next!'

'Well, suggestion number two...' Meg said slowly, and paused again.

'Out with it,' said Arthur.

'Landscape gardening.'

'Landscape whatting?'

'Your fingernails show that you're used to working with the earth,' she said. 'It could be just the thing for you.'

Arthur looked at his nails. 'I just ain't cleaned 'em for a while, is all.'

'Oh, I see. And gardening doesn't...grab you?'

'No. It doesn't. Come on, come on.' He snapped his fingers under her nose. 'I'm not getting my money's worth here.'

'I should warn you that I can only make one more suggestion for a single groat,' said Meg.

'One more? But the first two were rubbish.'

'They weren't rubbish, they were quality suggestions. Whether or not you choose to follow them is your affair.'

'Well, the last one better be a good'un or I'll be wanting that groat back.'

'I don't do refunds,' Meg said, and even though she smiled as she said it there was a look in her eye that warned him not to try anything.

Arthur was obviously no hero because he looked away. 'All right, but make this one value for money.'

Meg sat back on her stool and looked at him. 'You know, someone with your attitude—'

He clenched his fists and jaw. 'What attitude?'

'—seems to me ideally suited for a life of combat.'

'Combat?'

'Have you considered the lists?'

'Lists? You mean like in jousting?'

'Yes. You might be rather good at that. Naked aggression often wins the day at a joust. I've seen it time and again.'

'Only knights can enter tournaments,' said Arthur.

'That's true in principle,' said Mental Meg, 'but I've met many a man who claims to be a knight and is anything but. Say you're Sir Pratt Gore-Winkletop of Krapp-in-the-Woods and until someone invents the internet no one can check if such a knight or place exists at short notice.'

'Nah,' said Arthur Penn.

'Nah?'

'Even if I wanted to go in for a joust, there's two reasons why I couldn't apart from not being a knight.'

'And they are?'

He ticked off the reasons on his fingers. 'One,

I don't have no armour. Two, my horse is only fit for pulling ploughs. Three, I don't fancy going bottom over nipple on the end of a lance.'

'Good thing she didn't suggest a career as a mathematician,' I whispered in Saggy's ear.

'Is that it then?' Arthur said gruffly to Meg. 'Your final shot?'

'Oh, I'm sure I could come up with a few more for a further groat,' she replied.

Arthur wasn't having any. He jumped off the couch. 'On your broomstick, lady,' he snarled. 'Sheez, what a rip-off!'

I jerked Saggy away from the flaps so Arthur wouldn't catch me when he quit the tent. I heard a thump followed by curses as we clip-clopped away. He'd barged out and crashed into a group of passers-by and told them what he thought of them. Mental Meg had not been wrong about the aggression.

CHAPTER SIX

Sir Bozo was sitting outside the booze tent. Sharing his bench was a ragged old boy with a tangled grey beard (a real soup strainer) and the brightest blue eyes I ever saw outside of a doll.

'Where have you been?' Sir B demanded when I rode up on Saggy.

'Me or him?' I asked.

'You.'

'I was taking a look round.'

'Look round, *sire*.'

'Didn't I say that?'

'No, you did not.'

I slipped down from the saddle. 'Ah well.'

Sir B turned to his bench pal. 'Peasants these days. No respect for their betters.'

'And good luck to 'em, I say,' said the ragged old boy.

Sir B's eyes popped. 'You can't approve of such cheek!'

'I approve of *spirit*. Have you got spirit, lad?'

'Oodles of it,' I said. 'Can't move for it.'

The man leant closer. 'How are you in the ideas department?'

'Ideas department?'

'If you had to write a story, would you be able to think of interesting things to put in it?'

'I don't write that well.'

'Of course you don't, you're a peasant, but could you dream up a story if you had to?'

'The boy does nothing *but* dream up stories,' Sir Bozo chipped in. 'Do you know, he tells everyone he meets that I got him at a slave market in a buy-one-get-one-free offer.'

'You did,' I said. 'I was the free one.'

'It wasn't buy-one-get-one-free, it was two-for-the-price-of-one-and-a-half.'

I tossed Saggy's reins his way – sort of. 'Well, I was the half then.'

He dived for the reins and fell off the bench. 'I'd have been better off keeping the whole one,' he said, grabbing the reins and getting up. 'My wife got him in the divorce settlement.'

'Bit of spark to this one, though,' the ragged man said. 'Not downtrodden like most of the underclasses.'

'I try to downtread him,' said Sir B. 'Doesn't seem to work.'

'Feel up to giving me some imaginative input?' the man asked me.

'Imaginative input doesn't come cheap,' I answered.

He patted his pockets. 'Bit short of the readies just now, I'm afraid.'

'That's what you get for breaking out of the chokey in the middle of the night,' Sir B said to him.

'Breaking out of the chokey?' I said, suddenly interested.

The man frowned at Sir Bozo. 'I told you that in confidence, knight to knight over a warm ale.'

'Which I paid for,' said my boss.

'Since when did you have money to buy ale all round?' I asked.

He gave me the heavy eyebrow. 'Not that it's any of your business, but I keep a small stash for the necessities of life.'

'Like ale.'

'Yes, like ale. Thirsty business, jousting.'

'All you did was get on a horse and get off again,' I reminded him. 'You said yourself that it wasn't worth getting out of bed for a joust like that.'

'See what I have to put up with?' Sir B said to the man.

The man didn't answer him. Addressed me instead.

'The idea came to me one night while gazing through the bars at the guards playing dice at this little round table. Suppose that table was a lot bigger, I thought, and it stood in the great hall of a wonderful castle, and noble knights sat round it instead of belching prison guards, and they set out on these amazing quests and things.'

Sir Bozo laughed. 'Noble knights, amazing quests? No one wants to read about things like that!'

'Have you started this thing?' I asked the man.

'Well, no, not quite. I need that input I mentioned to get me going.'

'The free ideas,' I said.

'I could give you a part in it,' he offered.

'A part in your book?'

'A small part. A page, say.'

'I'd get a whole page?'

'I mean you could *be* a page. A very lowly one, at the beck and call of some valiant knight riding off to do something heroic.'

'No deal,' I said. 'I'd want to be a squire at least.'

'All right then, a squire.'

'That's the only way he'll get to be one,' Sir Bozo said. 'In a piece of pulp fiction.'

'Thanks for the drink,' the ragged man said to him. Then he got up and draped an arm round my shoulders. 'I have a few thoughts of my own,' he said, strolling me away, 'but I don't want to start writing and get stuck, so what I thought—'

'Hey, I need the boy here!' Sir Bozo shouted. 'I'm on again soon!'

'—was that I'd compile a list of noble deeds and knightly quests, add a dash of spooning for the ladies and some gore for the bloodthirsty, and bind the whole lot together in a poetical sort of way. I was running along the road thinking about all this when I came upon Billy Camelot's tournament here. "Ah-ha," I thought, "just the place to get me some material!".'

'Billy Camlot's,' I said.

'What did I say?'

'Camelot.'

He shrugged. 'A detail. As it happens, you're the first person I've met here who seems to have something resembling a brain between his ears.' He stopped walking abruptly. 'Tommy Malory of Newbold Revel at your service.' He did a little bow as he said this. No one, even an escaped jailbird, had ever bowed to me before. I rather liked it.

'Sir Tommy?' I asked.

'Well, yes, technically, but I only use the title with people I need to impress. It rather gets in the way when talking to the lower orders, I find.'

'It would.'

'I'm intrigued to hear how you came to be in a slave market.'

'My dad swapped me for a horse and the man he got the horse from sold me to a slave trader.'

Sir Tommy's eyebrows lifted over his bright blue eyes. 'Your father swapped you for a horse? But that's dreadful!'

'It's life. He needed the horse to plough the field he won in an illegal game of Snakes and Ladders.'

'What about your mother?'

'No, he only won the field.'

'I mean what did she think about him swapping you for a horse?'

'She wasn't around. She'd gone off with a stable hand by then.'

'A stable hand?'

'Not just his hand. Why were you in the chokey?'

'Oh, you don't want to know about that.' He seemed a bit embarrassed about this.

'I told you about me,' I said. 'Come on, what did you do?'

'What I did was make a run for it. Prison life never did suit me.'

'You've been inside before then?'

'Oh yes. And broken out more times than you've had hot dinners.'

'Twice would cover that.'

I gave him the swift once-over. With his shabby clothes and wild hair and beard, he certainly looked like a man on the run, but he didn't act like one. Talk like one either.

'So why do you keep getting put away?' I asked.

'Because I keep getting caught,' he said.

'For doing what?'

'Oh, nothing much. Just the odd trifling spot of high jinks.'

'What sort of high jinks?'

'A little bit of burglary here and there.'

I gaped. 'Burglary!'

'And horse-stealing.'

'Horse-stealing!'

'And the occasional sheep and herd of cows.'

'Sheep and herd of cows!'

'And raiding an abbey.'

'Raiding an abbey!'

'With a hundred or so acquaintances.'

'A hundred or so acquaintances!'

'And one or two other tiny things. Nothing to get in a stew about.'

'Nothing to get in a stew about!'

'Apart from that murder charge maybe.'

'Murder charge!'

'It was an accident. The fellow should have ducked.' He sighed. 'A chap can't have a minute's fun these days without being incarcerated.'

'You've done all that and you're looking for story ideas? Why don't you just write about yourself?'

'Oh, no one would pay to hear about my sordid little life,' he said. 'People want stirring fantasies about chivalry and nobility and damsels rescued from dire situations. Now what do you say we see if you've got a few thoughts along those lines?'

I shook my head. 'Stuff like that's another world to me. Nearest I've come to any of it is the female Sir Bozo rescued a while back.'

'Sounds just the ticket. Tell me all about it.'

'Nothing much to tell. He hauled her out of a hedge she'd fallen into while drunk.'

'Oh. I was thinking of something a touch more menacing than hedges. Fierce beasts, giants, green knights who won't die even when you chop their heads off, that kind of thing.'

'Sorry,' I said. 'I've got nothing like that.'

He looked a bit downcast. 'I need to start my book very soon. If I don't I might shoot off on another escapade to relieve the boredom and end up swinging from a rope with very little joy.'

'Have you got names for any of your characters?'

'A few, for minor players. Why?'

'Well, good names could suggest interesting people, and once you have them you might find that you get ideas for the kind of adventures they would have.'

'It's a fair thought,' he said. 'Names...characters ...yes. That hedge-damsel. What was she called?'

'All I remember about her was that she was a grocer's daughter from Grantham with iron hair and a fake posh accent.'

'You don't recall her name?'

'Gwynn... Gwenny... Something like that.'

'Gwynn or Gwenny aren't very romantic.'

'Nor was she.' But then... 'No, wait.'

'What?'

'It was Guinevere.'

'Guinevere?'

'Yes. Definitely. I think.'

Sir Tommy skidded in his tracks, skidding me in them too because he'd gripped one of my shoulders again.

'Guinevere. What a name for a queen!'

'She was a drunk. In a hedge.'

'I'll miss that bit out. Queen Guinevere would be very sober and comely. Was the hedge-damsel comely?'

'She had a nose like a bridge.'

'Better miss that out too. Now if I can find a name for her king I might be getting somewhere. What's yours?'

'My what?'

'Name. If it fits, you could be Queen Guinevere's royal husband.'

'Bit young,' I said.

'Don't worry, married life will age you rapidly. I should know. Been there, done that, not bought anything T-shaped to commemorate it.'

I thought about this. A king would be a whole bunch of steps up from a squire, which would be a step or two up from a page, which would be at least half a step up from what I was now. Quite a promotion all in all.

'I accept,' I said.

'Accept?'

'The king job. I wouldn't have to be all lovey-dovey with this queen person, would I?'

'We're getting a bit ahead of ourselves,' Sir Tommy said. 'I need your name before I can make you my king.'

'Oh yes. It's Jiggy.'

'Jiggy?'

'Jiggy d'Cuer of Carboote-Sayle.'

'Jiggy,' he said thoughtfully. 'Unusual.'

'I got it from my dad.'

'Your dad was called Jiggy before you?'

'No, he called me that because the night I was born he danced a jig.'

'Oh, I see. He was happy.'

'Too right. For the first time in his life he had something to trade – when I was older, of course.'

'For the horse to plough the field he won in illegal Snakes and Ladders.'

'Yes. Do I get to be king?'

He stroked his ragged beard. 'Queen Guinevere and King Jiggy...'

'Works for me,' I said.

'King Jiggy and the Knights of the Round Table...'

I waited for the big offer. But then he shook his head. 'Guinevere is a high-born lady. She'd look down on someone called Jiggy – no offence – and his courtiers would laugh at him, and knights would refuse to sit round his table or fight for him. Have you got any other names?'

'No, just the one.'

'I mean other people's. Who do you know?'

I was disappointed. From a peasant to a king in the space of two minutes would have been something to write home about if I had a home. But here I was, as peasantish as ever.

'I don't get to meet many people,' I said. I felt a bit miffed actually.

'But you must know some names. Come on, Jiggy, think.'

Maybe it was because he'd put me on the spot but I couldn't come up with a single name. My head was as empty as a foot-baller's wife's.

'Non-human names any good?' I asked.

'Non-human? What, like Rover? King Rover. I think not.'

'I'm thinking of Sir Bozo's horse, Saggy.'

He wasn't impressed. 'I somehow doubt that Lady Guinevere would give her heart to a King Saggy.'

'It's short for Sagramor.'

'That's better,' he said. 'But I think Sagramor is more a knight's name than a king's.'

I shrugged. 'It's your book. I've got another horse's name too, if you want it.'

'Oh yes?'

'Percival.'

'Percival? Hmm... Oh, I say, a punch-up!'

Two men had just jumped the fence around the foot-ball field. The man in front was hugging the pig's bladder everyone had been chasing, and the man behind him carried a shield, which he brought down with a clang on the back of the first man's head. Man One fell forward, but when he didn't let go of the ball Man Two kicked him in the ribs and tried to rip it out of his arms like a true sportsman.

Forgetting all about me, Sir Tommy surged forward to cheer on the two foot-ballers beating each other even more senseless than they were already. He wasn't alone. People were swerving in that direction from all over.

I wasn't one of them.

CHAPTER SEVEN

I was on my way back to Sir Bozo when I bumped into Sir Wilfred d'Retch's squire, Ryan de Bryan. I asked him if he'd finished for the day.

'I'm just hanging about in case I'm needed,' he replied. 'Doubt that I will be. Sir Wilf's working on a poem to his lady-love, Nancy du Binte of Oiseau-dans-le-bain.'

'Quite a mouthful,' I said.

'Yeah. Glad it's not me that has to find a rhyme for that.'

'Is he booked for any more jousts?'

'Just one, tomorrow. He's not looking forward to it. Knows he couldn't beat an eight-year-old on a rocking horse.'

'Is that who he's up against?'

He gave me a peculiar look and went on his way.

I'd almost made it to the ale tent when I overheard two voices that I was getting to know better than I wanted to. It was a private chat that anyone with ears as sharp as mine could pick up if he happened to be loitering nearby pretending to be cloud-gazing. Spiv Merlin was holding Arthur Penn's collar in one hand and a magic ball in the other, and Arthur was squirming and saying, 'Leave it out, guv, I'm just an honest working man trying to grub a living.'

'You'll need to grub harder than that if you want to pick *my* pocket,' Merlin replied. 'I've been watching you, friend. Not doing too well today, are you?'

'Watching me? You been watching me pick pockets?'

'Watching you fail to. Are you sure you're suited to your current line of work?'

'Oh, don't you start.'

'Start what?'

'I'm not interested in a caring profession or gardening, all right?'

'I'd have been surprised if you were,' said Merlin. 'How about tilting?'

'Tilting?'

'Jousting.'

Arthur clutched his head. 'What do I have to do, wear a shirt with "I DO NOT JOUST!" on the chest? Will you let go of my collar please?'

Merlin let go of his collar, but gripped his arm so he couldn't run off. 'How would you like to improve your social standing?' he asked. 'Make a bit of dosh and maybe a reputation.'

'I've already got a reputation,' Arthur said. 'In the next county but one. That's why I'm trying my hand in this one.'

'Not too successfully, it seems. Have you got a horse?'

'I might have – why?'

'Just tell me.'

'Yes, I've got a horse.'

'Where is it?'

'Tied to that tree there.'

Merlin glanced towards the tree, and sneered. 'A carthorse?'

'Yeah, well, we can't all have magnificent stallions,' said Arthur.

'No, we can't *all*,' said Merlin. 'But you can.'

'Eh?'

'Stick with me, chum, and we could both leave

here quite a bit better off than we are now.'

'How?'

'Let's fetch your horse and find somewhere away from the crowd.'

I watched them walk away. I didn't know what Merlin was planning and didn't want to. All I hoped was that whatever it was, it tipped the pair of them nose first down the nearest toilet chute.

Sir Bozo's second joust of the day wasn't such a breeze as his first. His opponent was Sir Melton of Mowbray, who looked a bit pie-eyed to me, but he was an experienced knight who knew how to stay in the saddle in spite of the drink. Neither he nor Sir Bozo was the kind of knight audiences throw their hats in the air for, though. The really popular ones are young and fit, able to leap off horses in full armour and beat the chainmail pants off their opponents. Sir Boz and Sir Mel weren't young and fit, their days of leaping off anything were distant memories, and it soon looked as if neither one would triumph over the other. When they'd galloped down the lists four times without scoring any points against one another, they climbed down and started bashing away with their swords. They were about equal as swordsmen too, but they weren't all that quick, and after ten minutes of neither of them getting anywhere the audience started to heckle.

'Get off! Go 'ome!'

'You're both past it!'

'Go for the legs, they've almost 'ad it anyway!'

Sir Bozo won almost by accident in the end. Someone threw a dead rat at them, Sir Mel looked down to see what he'd stepped on, and Sir B's sword sent his shield flying. 'Victory! Victory!' the crowd bawled. 'Now get off, you doddering old losers!'

When I helped Sir Bozo out of his helmet he was sweating like a porker.

'I'm too old for this,' he said.

'Yup,' I agreed.

He scowled. 'You're supposed to say, "No you're not, sire, you have years of fantastic victories in you yet".'

'Yeah, but I have this new policy. It's called "always tell the truth even if it hurts the one you love".'

'Insolent whelp. Get me out of this gear.'

He clanked off to the changing tent and Saggy and I followed him.

In the tent I helped Sir B out of his armour. 'I used to soil these when I was younger,' he informed me when he was down to his long johns.

'Thanks for sharing that,' I said.

'I knew fear when facing an opponent back then. Not now. I'll wager there isn't a knight here that I can't beat.'

'It was a rat that did it for Sir Melton,' I reminded him.

He slapped me round the head. 'When I want your opinion I'll ask for it!'

When he was back in civvies we left his armour in a heap with a ticket on it for picking up later. Outside the tent, a few paces along, there was a stall packed with bottles, tubs and dodgy-looking gadgets. The mouth of the one-eyed man who ran the stall was down to one black tooth and one silver.

'Facelift, sire?' he asked Sir Bozo as we passed.

My knight juddered to a halt. 'What was that?'

'You could do with one, if I may say so,' beamed

the two-toothed one-eyed salesman. 'The sagging jowls add years that no ageing knight would care to admit to.'

'How would you like the point of my sword up your jacksie?' Sir Bozo enquired chivalrously.

'Ha-ha,' said the quack, like he'd heard that before somewhere. 'Also,' he added, 'the big fat sacks under your eyes. I can reduce those with my unique blend of goat and ox urine. Gotox, I call it. And if you fancy sexier lips while we're at it, I can insert wedges of dried poodle dung in them, though it's usually the ladies who go for that.'

Sir B looked like he was about to storm off in a rage. But then he hesitated. 'This facelift. What happens exactly?'

'I'm glad you asked,' the man said. He produced a huge pair of tweezer type things with two little hooks on the end. 'I strap you into that sturdy wooden seat there, stuff a rag in your mouth so your screams won't frighten the horses, and hook these Personal Facelifters into the skin just below the hairline.'

'Then what?'

'I tug like crazy. Once you've come round and

mopped the blood off, you'll be amazed how taut your skin is.'

'How much?' Sir Bozo asked.

I led Saggy to the stable tent, where hay was free for the mounts of the day's jousters, left him with the man in charge, and went for a wander. The stable tent was near the field the foot-ballers had been kicking the pig's bladder about in. There was no one playing now, but from the mess they'd left behind – litter, weapons, the odd body part – you'd think two armies had been hacking at each other for days. Over to one side of the field there was this tumbledown barn, which I headed towards thinking that maybe I could nap in it for half an hour or so. One of the barn's doors was half open and I was a quarter through it when I heard voices inside. I stopped. Listened.

'Now do you believe me?' one of the barn voices said.

'Oh boy, do I!' said the other.

The voices belonged to Spiv Merlin and Arthur Penn. There seemed to be no way to avoid those two today.

I clung to the shadow of the door and peered inside. The barn had two storeys, but most of the upper floor had caved in, along with part of the roof above it, so it was quite light in there. In the light stood a powerful-looking white stallion. Sitting astride the stallion was a man in shining golden armour. The 'Oh boy, do I!' had come from the armoured man.

Arthur Penn.

I was still wondering where they'd got such a great horse and armour when I noticed that Merlin was holding the magic balls he'd cheated his client out of. 'These babies are going to make you quite well off and me even richer than I am already,' he said.

'I don't get it,' said Arthur. 'All you did was bang them together.'

'And while I did that I told them to transform you and your carthorse into a wondrous knight and a glorious steed,' said Merlin.

'But that's...magic.'

'My, you're a bright one. Yes, friend, magic it is. And thanks to this magic you're going to knock people's eyes out.'

'I am? How?'

'You're going to be a surprise last-minute entry in today's tourney.'

'Me?' said Arthur.

'You,' said Merlin.

Arthur shook his helmet. 'I don't think so.'

'I do.'

'No, seriously. I've never been in a joust.'

'Ah, but this won't be just any joust,' Merlin said. 'This will be one you can't lose. Trust me. Trust my balls.'

'Sorry, guv,' said Arthur, starting to dismount. 'You got the wrong man.'

'Stay where you are!'

Arthur froze. 'Hey, come on,' he said, 'do I really look like the kind of bloke who can fight a knight?'

'That's exactly what you look like,' said Merlin. 'And that's exactly what you're going to do. Maybe more than one knight.'

'More than one?'

'If this works as well as I think it will, there'll be no stopping you. Today's joust will be just the start of things for us.' He grabbed a badly dented old shield that was leaning against the wall and banged the magic balls together while muttering something. Then, before his eyes and Arthur's eyes and my eyes and the magnificent stallion's eyes, the old shield became a brand-new one, white, with a rearing red dragon on the front.

'Your shield, Sir Knight.'

Arthur wasn't impressed. 'A dragon? That's a Welsh emblem, innit?'

'I believe so – why?'

'I'm not Welsh.'

'That was yesterday,' said Merlin. 'Today you're Sir Arthur Penn-Dragon of Merthyr-Tytfil.'

'Sounds a bit grand,' Arthur said doubtfully.

'It has to be. All-conquering knights can't come from somewhere like, say, Chiswick.'

'All-conquering?'

'That's you. Just one more thing and we're set.'

Merlin found a stick that looked like it had been used for stirring cowpats, and when he banged the magic balls together and muttered, the cowpat stick grew and turned into the finest lance ever.

'Now, just before we go and knock those eyes out...' Merlin said, handing the fine lance up to

Arthur. 'A castle fit for a great knight is in order, I think.'

He banged the balls and muttered once more, and suddenly I was no longer standing in the shadowy doorway of a dilapidated old barn, but at the entrance to a great hall, with smart shields and flags and crossed swords all around the walls.

'Odds bodikins,' I said, or something just as medieval.

Unfortunately, this was overheard. Merlin and Arthur looked my way. So did the magnificent stallion. The stallion was the only one that didn't scowl.

'Oi, you,' Merlin said. 'Clear off.'

'It's me,' I said. 'You know me.'

'I know I know you. Get out of here before I turn you into a fly and swat you.'

I went. In a hurry.

CHAPTER EIGHT

When the last-minute entry rode into position a little later a gasp went up, mostly from the ladies in the stands. Even I had to admit that Arthur looked pretty gaspworthy in his golden armour on his beautiful white stallion, holding his fantastic shield and lance. He kept his visor down, which had to be his manager's idea. Merlin was a smooth operator. He knew that if anyone saw the weasel-eyed phizog inside that helmet they'd be turned right off. When Arthur unseated his first opponent right away, it was probably a bigger surprise for him than for anyone watching. Because they liked the way he did it and the way he looked, the crowd shouted for more of the same – and Merlin saw to it that he gave them more. A lot more. Challenger after challenger fell to his mighty lance. Soon people were calling him the Golden Knight, and hot maidens and dumpy wives were running into the lists between jousts to stuff ribbons into gaps in his armour, and little notes with their addresses and bodice sizes.

'I used to be like that,' Sir Bozo said of the Golden Knight. 'When I had a castle, social standing, a decent suit of armour.' He sighed. 'Those were the days.'

'And knights,' I said.

He looked so sorry for not being what he said he was once upon a time that for a second I felt sorry for him too. But then I remembered that he was still a Sir, with his own shed and allotment, while I was just an unpaid dogsbody with nothing at all and no title except peasant.

'What was his name? Didn't catch it.'

This wasn't Sir Bozo, it was Tommy Malory, who'd just joined us.

'Well, *today* it's Sir Arthur Penn-Dragon,' I said.

The three of us watched the pickpocket in golden armour topple his latest challenger and ride back to his end with head and lance held high. 'I've seen enough,' Sir Bozo said, and toddled off to sulk. The Golden Knight was mopping the floor with everyone who went against him, stacking up points without effort, which meant Sir Bozo would struggle to make even second place, especially with only two jousts booked for the morrow.

'Cool name for a king,' Sir Tommy mused when Sir B had gone.

'What is?' I asked.

'Arthur Pendragon.'

'You're still talking about your book, right?'

'Of course. Queen Guinevere and King Arthur. Good combination.'

'You can't call your king "Arthur",' I said. 'Sounds like someone who sells hooky gear off the back of a cart. You might as well call him...I don't know...Alfred.'

'Been done,' said Tommy. 'Any idea who that is whispering to him?'

The Golden Knight was leaning down in the saddle while Merlin spake into his armoured ear.

'That's Spiv Merlin.'

'Merlin?'

'*Spiv* Merlin.'

'Another good name.'

'Spiv?'

'Merlin. Some sort of counsellor to the king perhaps?'

I smirked. Couldn't help it. That crook Merlin, counsellor to a king.

'Why stop at counsellor?' I said with a chuckle. 'Why not make him a magician?'

Sir Tommy glanced at me in surprise. 'A magician?'

'Yeah. He does all this magic stuff to help King Arthur win battles and things.'

I thought he would say that he'd never heard such a rubbish idea and drop the whole thing. But a broad grin broke out in the general region of his lips.

'Brilliant!' he said.

My chuckle died and my smirk fell to the deck with an unhearty clunk.

'I was joking,' I said.

He must have missed that bit, for he clapped me delightedly on the shoulder. 'I was right about you, Jiggy. You're full of ideas.'

'Full of something anyway,' I said, and hunched away looking for something to kick.

What got me, what really stewed my prunes, was that if Sir Tommy wrote his book and made Arthur king and Merlin a magician, those two could become famous. But then I had another thought.

A much better one. Tommy had led a life of crime and spent a good chunk of it locked up, and because he didn't seem able to help it he would probably do something antisocial again before long and be shoved back inside, and next time, because he wasn't exactly a spring chicken, he might have to be carried out feet first. Which would mean that he wouldn't get a chance to write his book.

That cheered me up quite a bit actually.

It was almost midnight and I was asleep on my straw-covered wooden bed above the swamp our floor was slowly turning into. *Crash.* Door thrown back. My lord and master, half-sozzled. He zigzagged across the squelchy floor, fell onto his knightly bed, put his old school sword on his chest, and started snoring. I tossed and turned for a bit while he grunted loud enough to bring the battlements down, but tossing and turning never gets me back to sleep, so after a while I got up, jumped into my tights and smelly old jerkin, and trudged through the bubbling mud to the door.

Things were still hopping at the tournament ground even though it was so late. Jugglers and jesters were still hoping to cop a coin or two, sharks were still trying to sell junk, and drunks were singing cheerfully as they fell over things. While strolling around, I came across Merlin's client, the tubby little man he'd cheated out of the magic balls. He was standing between a couple of tents banging my fake balls together and ordering them to do things. I was tempted to approach and say, 'It'll never happen, chum,' but I probably wouldn't have been thanked for my trouble, so I didn't. I was about to walk on when he said, 'Ah, sod it,' tossed the balls over his shoulder, and stormed away. I went and picked them up. Put them in my pocket. They might not be magical, but I'd made a good job of them and not been paid for them. Shame to just let them lie there to be trodden into the ground.

When I got bored walking round and watching people get ripped off, I turned homeward to give snoozing through Sir B's snores another shot. I was passing the field where Merlin had turned the dilapidated old barn into a castle when something happened that made me hoot. The castle wasn't enormous, like some of them are, but it was pretty smart, with turrets and battlements and all, and ivy growing up the walls like it had been there forever and a day. Earlier I'd heard people wondering how come there was suddenly a castle there when there hadn't been one before, but people don't like to worry about things they don't understand in case they get nightmares later, so there wasn't a huge fuss about it. What made me laugh as I was passing was that the castle suddenly shuddered and turned back into a barn. The nice little stable that had stood against the castle also turned back into what it was before – a rotting tree stump. The dusty old carthorse that had been inside the stable looked puzzled, like it was wondering if it had dreamed about being a magnificent white stallion.

I chuckled as Arthur Penn and Merlin stumbled out of the barn, dazed and full of sleep. Arthur was back in his original clothes and Merlin swung his cloak over the nightshirt he was wearing.

'What happened?' Arthur gasped.

'The magic wore off, that's what happened,' Merlin said. 'Well, at least we know now.'

'Know what?'

'That it isn't permanent. Still, no problem. We merely renew our subscription.'

He took the magic balls from the secret pocket in his cloak, banged them together, muttered, and the dilapidated barn was a really neat small castle once more. The stable was also back. Merlin banged the balls a second time, muttered again, and the carthorse turned back into the magnificent white stallion. I swear, if a horse can grin, that one did as it returned to its comfy stable.

Merlin started to go back into the castle.

'What about me?' Arthur said.

'I'll see to you in the morning,' Merlin snapped.

Arthur stuck his lip out. 'I want to be *Sir* Arthur again. Right now.'

'I've created a monster,' Merlin said, but gave in, and in a trice the weasel-eyed pickpocket was back in the golden armour.

Arthur clanked stiffly inside, and Merlin followed him and closed the door. I heard heavy bolts being drawn (or maybe painted).

It tickled me to think of Arthur standing up all night in his armoured suit, but I supposed a castle as swish as that had beds and he'd lie down on one.

I envied him that bed. I'd never had a proper bed, even at Sir Bozo's real castle before his wife got it. I sighed and set off for my hard wooden bed and mattress of prickly straw. But before I'd taken more than half a dozen steps I stopped. Looked back at the castle. If the place was fully equipped it might have more than two beds. Beds that weren't being used…

It wasn't hard getting in. All I had to do was climb the ivy to a first-floor window and wriggle through. The room I fell into had a chair and a rug, but that was all. I went to the door and listened. No sound. I slipped out, into a shadowy corridor. I found Arthur's room easily enough. The sound of him turning over gave him away. His door was half open, so I looked in. Saw his rigid form stretched out like a golden statue on a bed. He'd even left his helmet on.

I crept to the next door along. This one was closed. I put an ear to it. No sound from the other side, but Merlin might not be a snorer. I clenched my buttocks and turned the big handle, pushed the door back, daring it to creak.

It creaked.

I paused while the deafening sound of the creak died, then peeked round the door. There he was, in this enormous four-poster bed, curled up like a baby, thumb in mouth. I started to close the door, but it creaked sharply again, like it was saying 'I don't wanna be closed!', and Merlin grunted, so I left it as it was and hotfooted it down the corridor.

Round the next corner I found a room with a door that didn't creak and a bed with no one in it. I lugged the heavy chamber pot from under the bed – that castle had everything! – and put it a few inches in from the closed door so that if anyone barged in the crash would wake me and fling me out of the window before I could be caught by the scruff of the neck and beaten seven shades of what-have-you.

Oh, but that bed was soft! I'd never known such luxury. I just sank into it, and sank and sank, sighing with pleasure.

It was starting to get light when I woke with a start. This wasn't the sort of start you do when someone shoves your bedroom door back and hits your chamber pot. It was the sort that happens when, somewhere in your luxurious doze, you get an idea that jerks you into a sitting position saying, 'But of *course*! Why didn't I think of it *before*?'

I got out of my wonderful bed, used the chamber pot by the door, swished it aside, and headed on tiptoe for Merlin's room.

CHAPTER NINE

Sir Bozo put his name down for an extra joust on Day Two, hoping to make up some of the points he'd missed out on yesterday. He knew that whatever he did he couldn't get more points than the Golden Knight had already accumulated, but second place had to be better than no place in such a downmarket tourney. Our first tilt of the day was in the morning, and we were just about ready for it. I was on the steps beside the boss and Saggy, Sir B's helmet in my hands, when he caught sight of the knight he was going against.

'Another loser,' he sneered.

'You know him?'

'No, but I can tell what he's made of by the way he holds his lance. Are there no worthy opponents left?'

'There's the pickpocket in gold,' I said.

'Pickpocket?'

'Sir Arthur Penn-Phoney. You want a tip? Go against him this afternoon and you might just beat him.'

He looked at me. 'You really think I could hold my own against such a knight?'

'I hope so. There are some jobs even I won't do.'

I rammed his helmet down on his head.

'Mmmfffffssssssrrrrrggggg?'

I lifted his visor.

'I said where's he going?' he repeated, in English this time.

I looked along the lists. The knight he was booked to fight was turning his horse away.

'Probably forgot his packed lunch,' I said.

'Go and find out what's going on.'

I jumped down and ran at a crouch along the lists. At the other end I saw our opponent and his horse being replaced by another knight, another horse. The other horse was a magnificent white stallion.

'What are you doing up this end?' Merlin demanded.

'Trying to find out where that knight's schmoozing off to,' I replied.

'I have no idea. All that matters is that he's given his place to my man.'

'Why would he do that?'

'I dropped him a few groats.'

'You bribed him?' He smiled but said nothing. 'Oh, I get it,' I said. 'You want to see Sir B face down in the dirt with his bum in the air.'

His smile broadened. 'An attractive picture if ever there was one.'

'Isn't it enough that you've got his castle?' I asked.

'Not quite,' he said. 'There's one more thing of his that I want before I'll be satisfied.'

'His shed? His allotment?'

'Oh, he's welcome to those. No, I want the sword he won at school.'

'What do you want with that old thing?'

'Well, since you ask,' Merlin said. 'I was the brightest boy by far at our educational establishment. No one could trump me in any intellectual or academic exercise. I did reasonably well at sports too – except when up against Bozo. He beat me in every contest. The final straw was our last school sports day.'

'What happened on the last sports day?'

97

'He annihilated me in the toe-wrestling championship.'

'Toe-wrestling championship? You're pulling my leg. Or toe.'

'Not at all. Toe-wrestling is a traditional sport of we upper classes. You peasants have no idea how your betters live, have you?'

'Guess we don't,' I said. 'Oh, the loss. So young Bozo beat your toe into the ground, did he?'

'Yes. Literally. I still get pains in that toe when it rains.'

'And the prize for winning was that old sword?'

'That top-*calibre* sword.'

'Sure you don't mean toe-calibre?'

'The words "*top*-calibre" are plainly engraved on the blade,' he said. 'I want that sword. Always have. I'll never feel that I've completely triumphed over Bozo until I win it from him.'

'You won't win it in a joust.'

'Indeed. Sadly, for the present, I must content myself with seeing him humiliated. But I'll get the sword someday, somehow.'

I went back to our end, where I found someone spitting on Sir Bozo's cruddy old shield.

The spitter was Sir Wilfred d'Retch's squire, Ryan de Bryan. As I approached, he wiped the dollop of spit away with a cloth and rubbed the shield with an elbow. Sir B sat on Saggy watching him. Smiling.

'What's he doing here?' I asked.

'He's a squire,' Sir B said.

'Yeah, but he's not yours, so why's he spit-and-polishing your shield?'

De Bryan flashed his teeth at me. 'I was strolling by and thought your master's shield could do with a buff-up.'

'Buffing up his shield's not your job,' I said.

'No, it's not,' said Sir B. 'But when was the last time you did it?'

'I've never done it. I didn't know shield-buffing was in my slave description.'

'If you were any use at all you wouldn't need telling. But I suppose you have to be a professional squire to think of polishing a gentleman's shield without being told to.'

'Professional? He's only been squiring for a couple of days.'

Sir Bozo gazed approvingly at de Bryan. 'Such

a short time? I'm even more impressed. You have the makings of a first-class squire.'

'Why, thank you, sire,' de Bryan said, handing him the shiny shield.

'And he calls me *sire*!' Sir B cried, so joyfully that I thought he was going to clap his hands and burst into song.

'You can go now,' I said to de Bryan.

He ignored me, but bowed to Sir Bozo. 'Good day to you, sire. I hope we meet again sometime.'

'So do I, my boy, so do I,' gushed Sir B.

When the foot-ball-loving crawler had gone, Sir B asked me what I'd found out. I told him that he didn't deserve to know, but the knight he was booked to meet had sold his place to Merlin's man.

'Merlin's man?'

I climbed the steps beside Saggy. 'The Golden Knight.'

'Spiv Merlin is the Golden Knight's manager?'

'Yes, and Merl wants him to beat you to something vaguely pulpish.'

He went pale. 'You said you thought I might do well against him.'

'I said this afternoon. This morning you don't stand a chance.'

I slammed his visor shut.

When the trumpet blew, a herald announced that in a change to the advertised programme Sir Arthur Penn-Dragon would smash Sir Bozo de-Beurk into half a hundred pieces, maybe more.* Sir B's entire suit of armour quivered when he heard this. He didn't know it, but he could have been at least as good as Arthur with a little help from me. But I felt betrayed. The moment my back was turned he'd allowed his shield to be polished by someone who wasn't even working for him. 'Serve you right if you get trampled to a mass of blood, bone and rusty metal,' I muttered as he rode out.

At the first charge, Sir B swayed to one side as the two of them approached (maybe it was nerves) so that Arthur's lance only grazed his shield. But on the way back Arthur twitched the point of his lance towards Bozo's chest at the last moment and struck him right between the armoured man-boobs. Sir B flew backwards with a muffled yell that was followed by an unmuffled thud as he smacked the mud. Cheers and whistles for the

---

* Merlin must have paid the herald to say this. Wizard PR.

Golden Knight as he rode back to his end. Laughter and taunts for Sir Bozo as he limped back to ours.

'I'll never live it down,' Bozo wailed as I lifted his helmet. 'Laid low at such a tinpot tournament!'

'You didn't have to be,' I said.

'What do you mean by that?'

'Tell you later. Maybe. Depends how nice you are to me.'

I wanted to be alone for a while, but being alone at a busy event like that isn't easy and everyone and his brother's mother's uncle's aunt tried to sell me something or talk me into something as I sloped around. I wasn't interested in any of it, mainly because I was as skint as skint can be. What did interest me – a bit – was the two scowling men in uniform stopping people and showing them a picture. I wondered what that was about, but I wasn't so curious that I bothered to find out.

The second version of Merlin's little castle was still in the field where foot-ball had been played yesterday. Men and boys had turned up to play today as well, but the castle took up too much space so they kicked their ball against it instead. When they weren't kicking the inflated pig's bladder some of them took turns emptying their own, seeing who could pee the highest up the walls. One of them drenched the ivy I'd climbed up last night, so I went round the back and climbed up different ivy (dry) to another window.

Inside the castle I went downstairs in a hurry. The place could turn back into a barn any time and I didn't want to be upstairs when it happened in case I found myself suddenly on a bit of floor that no longer existed. I wasn't worried about bumping into Merlin and Arthur because I'd seen them getting ready to take on another knight after Sir Bozo. I was pretty sure Merlin wouldn't let Arthur stop after just one more victory either. But what he didn't know was that the days of Sir Arthur Penn-Dragon of Merthyr-Tytfil were seriously numbered. Why? Because in the early hours, while he was sleeping, I'd crept into his room and swapped his balls for mine. The balls now in Merlin's possession were the ones I'd carved and painted so brilliantly. I had the ones with the words 'Little' and 'Devils' on them. The magic ones.*

---

* These magic balls are the earliest known Little Devils products. Later Little Devils (not balls) appear or are mentioned in four of the adventures of Jiggy d'Cuer's 21st-century descendant Jiggy McCue. See *The Killer Underpants*, *Nudie Dudie*, *Neville the Devil* and *Rudie Dudie*.

CHAPTER TEN

When I told Sir Bozo what I wanted him to do, his eyeballs almost jumped out of his head.

'Joust with him again?' he said. 'Are you out of your *mind*?'

'Probably,' I said. 'But this time you'll beat him.'

'I can't beat him. No one can. He's better than anyone here, including me, sad to say.'

'He is now. He won't be after lunch.'

'Why won't he be as good after lunch?'

'He's a morning knight.'

'He did pretty well yesterday afternoon, as I recall.'

'That was Saturday. The rumour is that he's never at his best after Sunday lunch.'

'You shouldn't believe everything you hear, boy.'

'I don't. But this is for real. You can take him, boss.'

'Take him, *sire*.'

'My words almost exactly. Look, Sir B, here's

your chance to be the star of the show. You'd like that, wouldn't you?'

'Well, it would be rather nice to be celebrated after all these years in the wilderness,' he said. 'And even nicer to collect the champion's trophy at the end of the day. But Penn-Dragon's way ahead of the field. No one can accumulate enough points to beat him now.'

'Maybe not. But there's something else you could win. Something even more valuable – to you anyway.'

'What's that?'

'Never mind. Leave that to me.'

I left him wondering. If I'd told him what I had in mind he would probably cuff me round the ear and tell me to go and scrub something. That knight didn't deserve me.

I tracked Merlin to the VIP tent, where he and Arthur were tucking into leg of roast boar. I knew they were in there because there was a bunch of cross-eyed autograph hunters outside chanting, 'We-want-the-Golden-Knight, we-want-the-Golden-Knight!' and the security men on the flaps wouldn't let them in. I got past them by saying I was the Golden Knight's squire and that he'd summoned me.

Eating can't have been easy for Arthur because Merlin still wouldn't let him show his pasty face. He was sitting there lifting his visor just enough to slip one little piece of boar in at a time. Eating that way must have been such a boar.

'I have a challenge for you,' I said to Merlin.

His oily moustache twitched. '*You* have a challenge for *me*?'

'Sir Bozo does. He's told me to tell you that he wants to fight Sir Arthur again this afternoon.'

'What? After last time? Next time he might not get up again – ever.'

'I told him that. He wouldn't listen. I think it's the medication. Wait till you hear about the wager he's asked me to put to you.'

'Wager?'

'Yes. He says that if he wins he wants his castle back.'

Merlin laughed. 'That's absurd. Bozo has nothing to wager against it.'

'He has one thing,' I said. 'The sword he won at your end-of-term toe-wrestling championship.'

'The top-calibre sword? He'll wager that?'

'He will. Here's your chance to win it.'

He thought this over, but not for long. He didn't need to. He knew he couldn't lose. *Thought* he couldn't.

'Tell him he's got a deal.'

'He said you have to agree before witnesses.'

'Witnesses? He said that?'

'Yes. Cos he doesn't trust you to keep your word.'

Merlin chuckled. 'Fine with me. Call your witnesses.'

There were four other men in the tent, so I asked them if they would witness the agreement. One of them was one of the tourney judges. He had a very bad comb-over and hair growing out of his ears like weeds. When he and the other three were paying attention I made the announcement I'd been rehearsing.

'Hear ye.' (I've always wanted to say that.) 'This gentleman, Spivvel Merlin of Forever-on-the-Bog, hereby agrees that his noble knight, Sir Arthur Penn-Dragon of Merthyr-Tytfil, will tilt lances with Sir Bozo de Beurk this afternoon, and that if Sir Bozo wins Merlin will hand back the deeds of Sir Bozo's former castle. Do you so agree?' I said to Merlin.

'I agree my part,' he said. 'Now let's hear Sir Bozo's.' He said this like he thought Sir B was one huge joke.

'Sir Bozo has authorised me to speak for him,' I said in the same loud, clear voice. 'If he loses his tilt against Sir Arthur, he promises to give Merlin the top-calibre sword he won in a toe-wrestling competition yonks ago.' I turned to the witnesses. 'I call upon you four to swear witness to the terms of this agreement.'*

They didn't swear right away. They were puzzled. It was the comb-over judge who spoke up.

'A castle for a sword is hardly an equal wager.'

'It's a very special sword,' I replied. 'Isn't it?' I said to Merlin.

He smiled slyly. 'It is indeed. I look forward to possessing it.'

'Well then,' the judge said. 'I and these others duly witness the agreement.'

And the deal was done − without Sir Bozo knowing a thing about it.

---

* Boy, was I good!

CHAPTER ELEVEN

Sir Bozo hadn't followed my advice about putting his name down for another joust against the Golden Knight, so I did it for him and kept it to myself along with everything else. I slotted him into his armour well in advance of their bout because there was something I needed to do before they met.

'Why am I ready so soon?' he asked as I helped him up onto Saggy. 'I've got a good quarter of an hour yet.'

'There's a rumour the next joust will be cancelled and you'll have to go on early,' I said.

'You and your rumours. What's behind this one?'

'One of the knights has a runny nose. You know how messy it can get in your helmet when your hooter drips. Listen, I've got to nip off for a minute.'

'What?' he said. 'You can't just leave me sitting here like a...'

'Beurk?' I said.

'Exactly.'

'Go into a trance,' I suggested. 'You know the routine. Should do by now, it's one of those things you do really well.'

I darted round the back of the spectators' stands and raced to the other end of the lists, where I expected Arthur and Merlin to be. The Golden Knight had won his first joust after lunch and the buzz was that he was unbeatable. Arthur obviously thought so too by this time. He'd taken to strutting back and forth with his hand on his golden hip, helmet tilted so the sun caught it just so and made him look really heroic. But he and Merlin weren't where I expected them to be. I soon realised why when I saw the nose of a dusty carthorse sticking out from between a pair of tents. Peering past the nose, into the shadow that separated the tents, I saw Arthur, back in his old clothes and whining about it all going wrong, and Merlin scowling at the painted balls in his hands and demanding to know why they weren't doing what he'd told them to.

'We'll give 'em another go,' he said.

I took my own balls out in a hurry.

'Ready?' said Merlin.

'Ready,' said Arthur.

'Ready,' whispered I.

At the same instant that Merlin banged his non-magic balls together I banged my magic ones and whispered, 'Put Arthur in a suit of golden armour, but don't make him a great knight.'

Instantly, Arthur was back in the suit of golden armour, or one very like it. Merlin whistled with relief. 'Maybe I did something wrong last time,' he said. 'Still, we're all set now.'

'I don't feel the same,' said Arthur. 'Not as noble as before.'

'You didn't feel very noble the first time, as I recall,' said Merlin.

'No, but I did feel sorta different, and once I got into the lists I seemed to know what to do somehow.'

'As you will this time. Come on, I hear the herald bawling your name.'

'I'll need the gear,' Arthur said.

'Yes, so you will.'

Merlin went to the old stick and the dented shield they had with them and did the same thing with the balls, and I did it too, and lo, the stick was a fine lance and the beat-up shield was a smart white one with a dragon on the front. (The dragon I made was licking its tail instead of breathing fire, but they didn't notice.) I ducked back as Merlin turned to the sorry-looking carthorse. Waited till I heard the click of the non-magic balls before banging mine together and muttering what I needed to. Right away, the carthorse was a magnificent white stallion, tossing his mane and looking chuffed in a horsey sort of way.

'Off we go then,' Merlin said to Arthur.

I sped away, needing to get back to Sir Bozo before the joust started. As he was already helmeted and sitting on Saggy he didn't really need me, but I wanted to improve his knightliness with a spot of ball-banging so he'd win even more massively against Arthur. The old Bozo's gob would be well and truly smacked when Merlin returned the keys to his castle, and when he heard it was all thanks to me he would have to promote me to squire and, at the very least, give me a nice soft bed and my very own personal potty.

My progress back to the lists was slowed by all

the people heading for the stands to watch another Golden Knight joust. I was halfway there when a hand shot out of the crowd and gripped my arm.

'Jiggy!' It was Tommy Malory. 'I think they're onto me.'

'Who?'

'Pair of guards from the chokey I did a runner from. They're going round flashing a picture, which has to be of me.'

'Are you sure they're from the same chokey?'

'Oh yes, I know them: Galahad and Bedevere, two of the nastiest pieces of work I've come across in any jail. Do something for me, will you? Go and take a look at their pic and report back to me.'

'I can't,' I said. 'Not now. Sir Bozo's next joust's about to start.'

'Don't worry about him. I'll see him off for you.'

'The guards might notice you if you do.'

'No, they won't, I'll wear this.' He unrolled a bright-red hooded cloak he was carrying inside his own, and put it on.

'Where'd you get that?' I asked.

'A punter left it in the stands while he went for a warm canine sausage in some sort of roll.'

'It's a bit bright.'

'First thing that came to hand. Will you do this for me?'

'I would,' I said, 'but Sir Bozo's going against Sir Arthur Penn-Doodle again and—'

'He's going against the Golden Knight a second time?'

'Yes.'

'Is he insane?'

'He doesn't know it yet.'

'That he's insane?'

'Who he's fighting. I told him it was Sir Bors de Gannet.'

'Never heard of him.'

'You wouldn't've, I made him up.'

'Another good name for me to remember,' he said.

'For your book.'

He grinned. 'Yep. The ideas are coming thick and fast now!'

'Great. But please tell me that you've dropped Arthur and Merlin.'

'I've done no such thing. They're going to be my main characters. Look, help me out here. Please?

It won't take a minute. They're over there, talking to those plebs. Take a goosy-gander at the picture while I go and speed Sir Bozo to his ignominious doom.'

He pulled up the hood of his ultra-bright stolen cloak and headed listward before I could say no again. So much for my plan to make Sir B's win over Arthur really impressive! I shuffled across to the two prison guards thinking sadly that I would have to turn Tommy in. Unless he was locked away in some dim dark dungeon he would write his book about a king called Arthur and a magician called Merlin, and if the book caught on those two sleaze merchants would become famous, and that would just not be right.

'Hey, can I have a look at that?'

The guards turned. Scowled down at me.

'Don't mess with us, kid,' one of them said.

'I just want to see the picture,' I said. 'I might know the person you're looking for.'

'Oh yeah?'

'But if you don't want to show me...'

'Show 'im, Bedders. You never know.'

That was the other man. The one called Bedders

(Bedevere, obviously) hung the drawing in front of my eyes.

'Well? Recognise him? Careful how you answer now.'

'Why be careful how I answer?'

He bent down and put his big fat nose against my little thin one. 'Because if we think you're spinning us a line we'll beat the living wahoozah out of you. Get it?'

I gave him a big friendly grin. 'Think so. Want to say it again to be sure?'

He gritted his big yellow teeth and spoke slowly through them. 'Do. You. Know. This. Man?'

I eyed the drawing. It wasn't very good, but it was Tommy all right.

'I think so.'

'You think?' This was the other man, Galahad, who had a horrible great scar across the top of his nose.

'I'm sure.'

'Where'd you see him?'

'Right here.'

'At this tournament?'

'Yes.'

'I told you he'd be here,' Bedevere said to Galahad.

'He might be pulling a fast one,' the scar-nosed heavy replied. 'You know what these peasant kids are like.'

I bet you were pretty peasantish too before you got that job, I thought.

'But he might also be telling the truth,' said Bedders to Galahad. 'We have to check it out.'

'What will you do to him if you catch him?' I asked them.

'Cart him back to the chokey, where he belongs,' said Galahad. 'Then teach him a lesson for breaking out.'

'What sort of lesson?'

'Oh, the usual.' He looked fondly at his huge, bruised knuckles.

'You'll beat him up?'

'And down. And up again. One of the perks of the job.'

'When did you last see him?' Bedevere asked me.

'Yesterday.'

'What was he doing?'

'Riding away.'

It was a snap decision. I couldn't turn Sir Tommy

over to these bruisers, even to stop him turning Arthur and Merlin into heroes.

'Which way was he going?'

I jerked a thumb the opposite way to where Tommy was right now.

'What was he riding?'

'I think it was a horse.'

The noble Galahad smacked me round the head. 'What *colour*?'

I rubbed my poor abused head. 'Brown.'

'He didn't have the money to buy a horse,' Bedders said to his mate.

'He could've nicked it,' Galahad said. 'Anyone else see him ride off?' he asked me.

I shrugged. 'Have to ask them.'

'Who?'

'Anyone you like.'

He was about to say something else when this mighty clash of metal came from the lists, followed by an even mightier roar from the spectators. When the two guards looked towards these sounds I slipped smartly away.

I was nervous all the way to our end of the lists. Suppose that roar had been for Arthur unseating

Bozo? He might have, by accident. Or Merlin might have got to Saggy, stuck something in one of his hooves or under his saddle to put him off his stride. If Bozo was beaten he would have to give his old school sword to Merlin – Merlin could call upon our witnesses to the deal – and if that happened I wouldn't be able to show my face at Castle-de-Beurk-on-the-Allotment ever again. I'd be out on my ear without even a heap of straw to lay my weary head on.

CHAPTER TWELVE

Whatever I'd expected or feared to find back at the lists didn't match what was actually going on. Arthur's stallion and Saggy were wandering about chewing grass and their riders were on the ground, on foot, hammering one another with swords. Well, Sir B was hammering. Arthur was backing away and waving his sword like he was trying to swat butterflies. The crowd was going wild.

Tommy Malory was at our end like he said he'd be. You couldn't miss him in that bright-red cloak even though he was crouching down trying not to be seen. I zipped over and crouched beside him.

'What happened?'

'The most amazing thing,' he said. 'Sir Bozo and Sir Arthur charged one another in tried-and-trusted fashion and it was Sir Bozo whose lance made contact. Sir Arthur's was wildly off. Did you see the picture?'

'Picture?'

'The one Bedevere and Galahad were bandying around.'

'I saw it. It's you, no question.'

'Oh, my God.'

'Condolences. Why are Bozo and Arthur fighting on the ground?'

'At the second pass,' Tommy said, 'Sir Bozo knocked Sir Arthur clean over his saddle, reined in, slithered down, and helped him to his feet. But instead of showing gratitude, Arthur shoved him away, pulled his sword out, and set about him like a maniac.'

'I'm guessing Bozo didn't just stand there while he did that.'

'Oh no. He seemed rather taken aback, even with his visor down, but then he too unsheathed his sword. The Golden Knight's been backing away ever since. What did they say?'

'Who?'

'Galahad and Bedevere.'

'They said they want to drag you back to the chokey.'

'They said that? They said "drag", not "escort

politely, in a civilised fashion, have a good old laugh about all this when we get there"?'

'They might not actually have said "drag", but they're pretty keen to get their mitts on you.'

'Yes, they would be...'

We watched the fighting in silence for a minute. Arthur was younger than Bozo, but he was no more used to hand-to-hand combat than I was. When he lost his grip on his sword and it flew away from him, Bozo could have put him out of business then and there, but he dropped to one knee, picked up the sword, handed it back, and waited till Arthur looked about ready to carry on before starting to beat him about the arms and shoulders with the flat of his blade. Each new blow forced Arthur back another pace, and once again it was a one-way scene. The next time Arthur's sword left his hand it was deliberate. He threw it away. Then he yanked his helmet off and fell to his knees with his hands clasped towards Sir Bozo. The crowd gasped at this, really gasped. Or maybe the gasp was for their first sight of Arthur's pasty face and weasel eyes. Not only were these nothing like the features they'd been imagining inside that glorious armour, but they looked petrified.

'I'm going to have to be pretty inventive, writing about him,' Tommy murmured from the hood of his bright-red cloak.

'Make it easy on yourself,' I said. 'Forget about a king called Arthur. We'll come up with some other name.'

He shook his hood. 'I couldn't change his name now. But don't worry. I'll make something special of him, in spite of the appalling cowardice and lack of chivalry he's displaying here.'

I was just beginning to wish that I'd shopped him to the guards after all when someone shouted: 'My cloak! That person's wearing my cloak!'

A man in the stands was pointing at the crouching Tommy, which made several other people look our way too.

'I knew that cloak was a bad choice,' I said.

'I think that now would be an excellent time to make myself rather scarce,' said Tommy.

While the owner of the cloak fought his way through the crowd shouting, 'Stop thief!', Tommy gathered up the lower parts of it like a long dress and made a dash for it.

I turned back to the lists. The spectators were cheering Sir B, who was helping Arthur to his feet, and booing Arthur. Down the other end, Merlin was jumping up and down with rage. We'd won. Sir Bozo was going to get his castle back and I was going to be promoted to Knight's Favourite. I was about to trot along and ask Merlin for the castle keys when I had another of my wheezes, and ran back to the shed instead.

When I returned a few minutes later, I was surprised to see Sir Bozo and Arthur still in the lists. Sir B had his visor up and was turning round and round with his arms above his head while the defeated champ stood there drooping like his spine had been sent to the cleaner's. His armour was the only glorious thing about Arthur now, but because of the way he was standing even that didn't seem so impressive any more. I grabbed Saggy's and the white stallion's reins and walked them to their masters.

'I've still got it, son,' Sir B said to me. 'Still got it.'

'You've only still got it because this geezer's such a pathetic fighter,' I said.

This didn't please him all that much.

'Pathetic?' he said. 'After all his victories? No, he met a better knight, that's all.'

'And yesterday?'

'Yesterday he caught me off guard. Not today, though, not today. The crowd loves me. Look at them! They love me!' He noticed the sword I'd gone to the shed for and stuck in my belt. 'What are you doing with my old school sword?'

'I want Merlin to know what he's missed out on.'

'Missed out on?'

'Worry not, Sir Knight. Walk this way.'

'I have nothing to talk to Merlin about.'

'Don't worry, I'll talk enough for both of us.'

I gripped one of his elbows and tugged it. He shook me off, but followed, walking backwards, arms in the air for his admirers. Arthur came too, kicking his helmet ahead of him like a sulky little kid.

Merlin looked about as cheerful as a smoked kipper when I marched up to him with my hand out.

'Keys please, Louise.'

'I don't know what happened out there,' he growled, tugging one end of his long moustache, 'but someone pulled a fast one.'

'Like you didn't before, I suppose,' I said.

'No idea what you mean.'

'Of course you haven't. The keys.'

He reached inside his cloak and yanked out the big keyring I used to know so well. But he didn't drop it into my hand.

'I have personal belongings to get out of there first.'

Sir Bozo, following slowly, had missed the conversation, but he saw the keyring.

'Are they the keys to my castle?' he asked as he joined us.

'They are,' I said. 'And as soon as your old chum here's got his stuff out, they're yours again. So are the locks they fit.'

'What nonsense are you talking, boy?' Bozo said fiercely.

I was about to explain when the sound of a boot on metal got in first. Merlin's boot, Arthur's golden leg.

'Idiot!' he yelled in an ear-piercing high-pitched voice. 'How could you lose so completely? How could you lose at *all*?!'

'It didn't work this time,' Arthur said. He didn't seem so cocky now.

'Didn't work?' Merlin screeched. 'Look at your armour! Look at your horse! You must be a particularly useless specimen for such magic not to work on you two days' running when it worked on bits of old wood and a carthorse!'

'What's this about magic?' Sir Bozo asked.

'Don't you worry your unpretty old head about it,' I told him. 'Just be grateful for what I've done for you.'

'What you've done for me?'

'Got your castle back for you.'

'The castle's really mine again?'

'Yep. Feel free to reward me any time you feel like it.'

'But how could you have got it back for me?'

'Later,' I said, tugging his old school sword out of my belt and holding it up before Merlin's eyes. 'This is what you'd have got if your Golden Knight had done a better job.' I wanted to rub it in. He deserved it.

He stared at the sword like it was the first time he'd seen it. 'That isn't the top-calibre sword from school.'

'It is, isn't it?' I said to Sir Bozo.

'Indeed,' he answered.

'But it's so small,' said Merlin.

'You're probably bigger than you were when Sir B won it,' I pointed out.

'And...unimpressive.'

'He doesn't look after it, just sleeps with it on his chest, probably because Lady Ratfa...his former wife...got his teddy bear in the divorce.'

'All these years I've been thinking of it as a top-calibre sword like it says on the blade,' Merlin said. 'But if this thing ever had any calibre it's well and truly lost it. It's about as ex-calibre as a sword could be.'

'Excalibur...' said another voice. 'Good name for a sword.'

Tommy Malory had crept up behind us. He was in his normal clothes again.

'What happened to the hard-to-miss-in-the-dark cloak?' I asked.

'I dropped it over a drunk stretched out on the ground. Last I saw of it, the man I borrowed it from was beating it with a club.'

'With the drunk underneath it?'

'He didn't seem to mind, though being already

semiconscious might have helped there. What goes on here?'

'This lowly servant,' Sir Bozo said to him, 'claims to have negotiated the return of my castle.'

Merlin frowned. 'Are you saying you didn't know about the wager?'

'Wager?' said Bozo.

'The kid said he was representing you.'

'I was,' I said. 'I just hadn't told him, that's all.'

Sir Bozo's jaw fell on its hinge. 'Are you saying you wagered the sword against my castle?'

'It was all you had,' I reminded him.

'But if I'd lost I'd have had nothing at all!'

'But you didn't. You won, big time. So the castle's yours again.'

'No, it isn't,' said Merlin.

He was grinning meanly. That grin made me uneasy.

'It is,' I said. 'He won, fair and square.'

'But he didn't make the wager. He knew nothing about it. So the old place is still mine.'

'I'm not sure the witnesses would back you up on that,' said I.

'Witnesses?' said Sir B.

'One of them was one of those judges over there. The one with the sad hair and bushy ears. Merlin swore before him and three others that if you beat Sir Arthur in the lists he would return your castle.'

'Oh, did he now?' said Bozo.

'I'd offer to fetch the judge for you, Jiggy,' Tommy whispered in my ear, 'but I need to keep my head down.'

'I think you're safe now,' I whispered back. 'I told the guards I saw you riding away from here yesterday.'

'Very good of you. But they can't have believed you, because I saw them still prowling around a few minutes ago.'

'Really? Well, sorry, did my best.' I turned back to Merlin. 'I'll come and give you a hand to pack your gear, shall I?'

His mean grin had gone. He was beaten, and he knew it.

'Tell you what, though,' Bozo said to him. 'Seeing as you've coveted this sword for so long, I'll be generous. You can have it.'

Merlin frowned suspiciously. 'You'll give it to me?'

'I will,' said Bozo.

I was as stunned as Merlin. 'But it means so much to you,' I said. 'You've slept with it on your chest every night since you lost the castle.'

'That's because it was all I had left. But now that I have my castle back...' – he gave a hearty guffaw and snatched the old school sword from me – '...this piece of trash is all yours, Spivvel Merlin!'

He raised his arm and chucked the sword as far as he could. Over and over it went, blade over hilt, hilt over blade, to finally land point down in the big dark heap that Billy Camlot's Equine Ordure Technician had built with the horse droppings he'd been carting there from all over the site. The sword stood there, quivering dramatically.

'Oh boy,' murmured Tommy Malory in awe.

'What now?' I asked.

His blue eyes were shining brighter than ever. 'Imagine if that stuff solidified,' he said. 'And there was this notice carved into it that said something like "Whomsoever can pull this sword from this heap of manure is the rightful king of this land".'

'The book?' I said.

'Always,' he said. 'Oh, it's going to be great. Great!'

'So's this,' said a deep voice as two big hairy hands slapped on Sir Tommy's shoulders from behind.

One of the hands belonged to the scar-nosed prison guard, Galahad. The other belonged to his equally horrible co-worker, Bedevere.

'Oh no,' said Tommy.

'Oh yes,' said Galahad. 'Nobbled, my son. It's back to the chokey for you, where I have it on good authority that you'll stay till you rot.'

Tommy sighed philosophically. 'Ah well, I've had a fair run.'

'You have,' said Bedevere, 'and you'd better not try it again, mate.'

Galahad bent Tommy's arm up behind his back and marched him away.

'Bye, Jiggy!' Tommy called as they went. 'Thanks for all the input!'

'Any time.'

I said this through my fingers so the guards wouldn't realise it was me who'd tried to misdirect them. I was sorry to see Tommy arrested, but by the sound of it he'd have a hard time breaking out again, so with any luck he'd be inside till he was too old to write his name, let alone an epic about two great heroes called Arthur and Merlin.

'While you help Merlin clear his things out of my castle,' Sir Bozo said to me when Tommy and the guards were gone, 'I'm going back in the lists. My public is calling.'

They were too. 'Bozo! Bozo! Bozo!' they were shouting, just as the day before they'd shouted 'Arthur! Arthur! Arthur!' until the Golden Knight picked up his lance again and defeated another challenger, and another, and another.

'Are you sure that's a good idea?' I asked my knight.

His brows came down. 'Of course it's a good idea. I defeated the people's champion, which makes me the new favourite. I can't disappoint my adoring fans.'

I helped him up onto Saggy, who sagged as usual and looked like he was thinking, 'Next time I'm coming back as a *wasp*.' As Bozo rode back into the lists waving like royalty, Merlin pulled out the balls that didn't have 'Little' and 'Devils' on them and banged them together while muttering. I don't know what terrible thing he wished on Sir B, of course, because nothing happened. Merlin banged the unmagic balls again, muttered again. Still nothing. He glared at them.

'Why won't you work any more?' he said.

'Maybe they're fed up of being banged together,' I said. 'I'm pretty sure my balls would be.'

After Arthur and I had helped Merlin haul his gear out of the castle and load it onto a handcart, Merlin threw the keys to the ground.

'Not a great loser, are you?' I said, picking them up.

'Grrr,' he said.

'Do a good dog impression, though.'

We pushed the cart to the lists. I was surprised Merlin wanted to go back, but it turned out that he had his reasons. One was that he hoped to see Bozo toppled in combat, but he didn't get to see that because it had already happened. Sir B had won his first joust after we left him, but the next knight unseated him and walked all over him – literally – while he sprawled on the ground. This knight called himself Sir Asbo FitzBlighter the Mighty Smiter. The crowd loved Sir Asbo. They were already rooting for him and booing Bozo when we arrived.

'Gadzooks, they're a fickle lot,' Sir B grumbled as he limped over to us.

'Look on the bright side,' I said. 'You've got your castle back. That has to be better than being a champ at a crummy do like this.'

'Castle *and* champ would've been nice,' he muttered.

'Now that's just pigging greedy,' I said.

'Pigging greedy, *sire!*'

I held out the keys. 'Here. And don't forget who you have to thank for getting the old pile of stones back.'

He narrowed his eyes at me. 'That was a very risky stunt you pulled,' he said.

'But it paid off.'

'You could have lost me my one last treasured possession.'

'Is that the same last treasured possession you called trash and tossed into a heap of manure? If so, you might be interested to hear that it's no longer there. Someone's nicked it.'

The other reason Merlin wanted to go back to the tournament was to see if any knight would manage to top Arthur's points. He needn't have worried on that score at least. Arthur had done so well before he lost the magic touch that he ended the day a bunch of points ahead of the next biggest scorer. Sir B didn't even get the second place he'd been aiming for, so he wasn't in a great mood when he rode off on Saggy to bang his head against the crumbling ancestral walls I'd got back for him.

I stuck around to watch the award ceremony. Arthur was still wearing the golden armour minus the helmet when he went up to collect his trophy. He'd lobbed the helmet into the foot-ball field that no longer contained a castle and some boys were jumping on it, trying to flatten it. Arthur shuffled up the steps to the little podium where a skinny maiden in a pointed hat smiled like she had a big fish bone stuck sideways in her mouth.

'Congwatulations, Sir Arthur, on a twuly tewiffic display of pwowess,' said the pointy-headed maiden.

'Give it here and cut the cwap!' said Arthur, snatching the trophy and storming back down.

The trophy was a large silver cup half full of coins. The silver wasn't great quality and the coins were mostly foreign. Merlin snatched the cup from Arthur, threw a handful of the coins at his feet, and said that was all he was getting for letting him down. Arthur looked like he would throttle him, but Merlin pulled out the fake magic balls and said, 'Go on, I dare you!'

'I'm not scared of them,' Arthur spat. 'They don't work no more.'

'They might not be able to keep turning pathetic little wimps into great knights,' Merlin spat back, 'but I'm sure they'll have no trouble turning them into even lower life forms that can easily be crushed underfoot.'

For a second Arthur looked like he would chance it, but in the end he backed down. Turned to the nearest peasant and smacked him round the head instead. Guess who the nearest peasant was.

CHAPTER THIRTEEN

Well, Sir Bozo didn't give me a nice big bed in a nice big bedroom in the family castle. But he did give me something.

'The boot?' I said when he told me. 'You're sacking me?'

'I prefer to say "dispensing with your services",' he replied.

'But you're showing me the door?'

'And the drawbridge. You're no longer needed. I have a real squire now.'

'Since when?'

'Since the last time you gave me some of your lip.'

'When was that?'

'The last time I saw you.'

And who should step out of the shadows but...Ryan de Bryan.

'What about Sir Wilfred?' I said to him.

'He lost his third joust and said he never wanted to fight another,' de Bryan said. 'Rode home vowing to devote his life to love and poetry. I didn't want to sit beside him while he did that, so I offered myself to this noble knight, who very kindly accepted me as his squire.' He bowed to his new boss. 'Rest assured, I will serve you well, sire.'

Sir B looked like he would burst with pride at these words. Pity he didn't. 'Now *he* has the right attitude,' he said to me out of the side of his mouth. 'Something you never had.'

'You never paid me to have the right attitude,' I said out of the side of mine. 'You have to pay squires, you know.'

'I'll pay him when we've topped up the de Beurk coffers a tad or two.'

'And how are you going to do that?'

'We'll enter some jousts. Good jousts, where the prizes are worth having.'

'I look forward to that, sire,' said de Bryan, who'd been earholing my private conversation with my ex lord and master.

'Creep,' I hissed.

He laughed, said he would go and polish Sir Bozo's armour until it could be used as a mirror, and left us alone.*

'What am I supposed to do?' I asked him.

'Up to you,' he said. 'You have an hour to pack your bags.'

'I haven't got any bags.'

'Then you have a minute and a half.'

'I can't believe you're doing this,' I said. 'You'd still be without this castle if not for me.'

'I'm not entirely unappreciative of that,' he said.

'Could've fooled me.'

'And to prove it…' He handed me a big rusty key.

'What's this?' I asked.

'The key to the shed.'

'So I see. Why are you giving it to me?'

'Why do you think? It's yours now.'

'The key?'

'The shed. And the allotment. I no longer need them now that I have my castle back. Now get the hell off my property before I set the dogs on you.'

'You haven't got any dogs.'

'I'll rent some.'

---

* A direct descendant of Ryan de Bryan – the football-mad Bryan Ryan – appears in many of the Jiggy McCue books. Ryan is Jiggy's archest enemy.

I saw Merlin just once more, and that was one time too many. He was standing under a tree banging his non-magic balls together and shouting, 'Work, damn you, work!'

'Problem?' I said.

'Yes, I've got a problem,' he snapped. 'These things are useless.'

'Maybe you have to be a magician to make them work.'

'I made them work before.'

'That was just after the actual magician handed them over. Perhaps there was still a bit of his magic on them then, and it's worn off.'

He frowned. 'You know, you might have something there.'

'So what you want to do is catch up with him and get him to sprinkle some more of his magic on them. Either that or enrol him as a sort of magical sidekick.'

Merlin looked about him. 'I wonder which way he went...?'

'I can tell you that,' I said.

He looked sharply at me. 'You can? How?'

'He came back after he went the first time because he'd forgotten his nostril plucker or something, and then he went that way.' I pointed in a direction that became quicksand after half a mile. 'He can't be more than a day's walk away. You might catch him if you shift yourself.'

'By Jove's insane old Aunt Nelly I think I'll do that!' Merlin cried, and without a word of thanks kicked up his heels and set off in the direction I'd suggested.

'Byeee,' I whispered, not waving fondly.

That night at Castle-d'Cuer-on-the-Allotment I slept in Sir Bozo's vacated bed, which was almost pure luxury after my heap of straw. But I woke with an odd feeling, wondering if a proper bed and no master to slap me round the head at the drop of a helmet was enough for a growing lad. I was young, I was free, I had my whole life ahead of me rather than behind me. Did I really want to spend my days eating cabbages full of slugs and peeing in a moat?

Later that morning I was sitting cross-legged on my drawbridge carving a commemorative plaque that I planned to sink into the middle of the field where the tournament had taken place. I'm not too good with words, so it was taking a while, but I'd almost finished when a shadow fell across me and a gruff voice spoke.

'What's occurring, son?'

I looked up. Arthur Penn, pasty-faced and weasel-eyed as ever, no longer in golden armour. Tucked into his belt was Sir Bozo's old school sword. So that's where it went. He also carried a spear that looked quite a bit too rich for him.

'Nice spear,' I said as a change from saying 'Good morning, nice to see you, how are the boils on your bum?'

'Good, innit?' he said, hoisting the spear. 'Found it on the tourney site after everything'd been carted away. I call it Ron.'

'Ron? You call your spear Ron?'

'Mm. Has a ring to it, doncha think?'

'It has something. I thought you'd be long gone.'

'Nowhere to go really. Nowhere special.' He eyed my shed. 'Quite a place. Thought so the very first time I clocked it. Who's it belong to?'

'Me,' I said.

He gaped. 'You? How come?'

'I'm royalty in disguise.'

'Boy, what I wouldn't give for such a gaff.' He eyed it some more. 'I never had a home of me own.'

'So make me an offer.'

'I would,' he said, 'but all I got is the few foreign coins that toad Merlin threw me and a dozen groats I lifted from a couple of purses around dawn.'

'Now there's a coincidence,' I said. 'This highly desirable residence, with its state-of-the-art swamp floor and own slug-infested allotment, is on the market for one dozen groats and a few foreign coins thrown by a toad.'

'You're kidding.'

'Would I kid a kidder?'

'Wow!'

He cradled Ron the Spear in the crook of his crookish arm and emptied his pockets. Handed me every coin he had. I hadn't been serious, but no one ever put so many coins in my palm before. Suddenly I was rich. By humble peasant standards anyway.

'Is that supposed to be a moat?' Arthur asked of the trickle of yellow water with flies *zzz-zing* above it.

'A young one,' I said. 'To make it grow you'll have to drink a lot and pee a lot.'

'Rather that than lance a lot,' he said with a weasel-eyed smirk.

After handing over the rusty key I went to the field where the tournament had taken place, and sank my commemorative plaque into the earth. These are the historic words I'd carved into it.

ON THIS SPOT, IN 1464, NOTHING HAPPENED

Then I set off to start my new life. I had a pocketful of groats and foreign coins, so I wouldn't go hungry for a while. And I had something else too. Two somethings. I took them out and held them, one in one hand, one in the other. Then I tossed them in the air and caught each one in the opposite hand. I tossed them again, caught them again – and again, and again – and inside of fifteen minutes I could have passed for a professional juggler. It was a good feeling, having a profession.

I walked off into the big wide world, juggling my Little Devils.

My balls, I mean.

The magic ones.

Jiggy d'Cuer

HISTORICAL NOTE

There's no real evidence that there ever was a king called Arthur, but it's thought that a powerful warlord of that name might well have fought great battles in 6th-century Britain. In *Jiggy's Magic Balls* I make out that Tommy Malory was the originator of the tales of Arthur and his knights, but many of these existed for quite some time before Malory's day. No less than four Tom Malorys have been put forward as the man who retold those old stories and added a few new ones, but the Sir Thomas of Newbold Revel is generally considered the most likely, so I've gone with him. The title Malory intended for his eventual book was *The hoole booke of kyng Arthur & of his noble knyghtes of the rounde table*, but by the time it was published in 1485 and given the slightly snappier title of *Le Morte d'Arthur* (The Death of Arthur) he wasn't around to throw a tantrum.

The colourful life which Sir Tommy describes to Jiggy was pretty close to that of the actual man. Born in the early 15th century of a well-to-do landowning family, Thomas Malory spent much of his teens at war with France (not all by himself, you understand) and in his early twenties was described as a country landowner with an interest in politics. Married and knighted by the age of twenty-five, the first indication that he might not have completely settled down came in 1443 when he was charged with wounding, imprisoning and stealing from a man named Thomas Smythe. Yet Malory must have had friends in high places, for he survived that small indiscretion and, that same year, became a justice of the peace and Member of Parliament.

A period of respectable political life followed, until in January 1450 Malory and twenty-six others ambushed and robbed one of the wealthiest and most influential men in the country: Humphry Stafford, Duke of Buckingham. This seems to have been a turning point, because from then on Malory committed felony after felony and did time in numerous jails. One of his most notable escapades again involved Buckingham. According to records, Malory and some accomplices stole seven cows, two calves, 335 sheep and a cart, and when the Duke went after him with a sixty-man posse, Malory raided his hunting lodge, killed his deer, and caused extensive damage. He was eventually arrested and imprisoned in Coleshill Manor, but he escaped by swimming the moat, and over the next forty-eight hours twice broke into Combe Abbey (the second time with about a hundred chums), insulted the monks, and took off with a great deal of money and goods.

In January 1452 Malory was confined to the Marshalsea Prison in London, but was bailed out several times while awaiting a trial that never came, possibly because jurors weren't all that bothered about turning up. During one of these bail breaks he and a friend went on a horse-rustling expedition across East Anglia and ended up in Colchester Jail. I don't know what happened to his pal, but Malory escaped almost immediately, only to be recaptured and returned to his London cell.

The list of misadventures goes on, as do the spells in one 'chokey' or another, from which he did a runner whenever he could, sometimes by bribing the guards. Malory is thought to have started his tales of *'kyng Arthur & of his noble knyghtes of the rounde table'* in one prison and to have finished it in another some years later, shortly before his death in 1471.

Jiggy d'Cuer would have been appalled to learn that Arthur and Merlin would become famous in spite of Sir Thomas's recapture at the tournament.

HYSTERICAL NOTE

In Arthurian mythology King Arthur's sword Excalibur wasn't the only weapon to bear a name. His shield is most often called Pridwen, his knife Carnwennan, and his spear...Ron. Yes, Ron the Spear. That's one thing I didn't make up.

ARTHUR PENN'S PLACE

For three weeks after he moved into the shed on the allotment Arthur the pickpocket peed night and day into the moat to try and raise the level, but it was clearly more than a one-man job, so he picked some more pockets and paid a gang of local yobs to help him out. He needn't have wasted his stolen money, for about two months after he took up residence the swampy floor burst and the shed sank. The theory is that the nearby river had been trickling into a sort of underground basin for years and that the basin had filled to overflowing and there was nowhere for the excess water to go but up. In no time at all, the area within the would-be moat became a substantial pond which, in homage to the sterling efforts of the shed's former residents, became known as Piddle Pond. If you would like to hear about something dramatic that happened at Piddle Pond a hundred and eighty-odd years after it came into being, look out for a Jiggy's Genes tale about a 17th-century Jiggy, *Jiggy and the Witchfinder*. To read of something even more spectacular that occurred there in the present day see the Jiggy McCue story, *The Meanest Genie*.

Michael Lawrence

PS. It is not recorded what happened to Arthur Penn.

JiGGY

THE VAMPIRE SLAYER

AS TOLD BY THE EDWARDIAN JIGGY

My first names are Jerome Ignatius Granville, but I call myself Jig for short and Jiggy for long, and can you blame me? I wish I could do something about my double-barrelled surname too. The first part of the barrel is my mother's maiden name, Offal, which she pronounces 'Orful' because she's a snob. The second part, my father's family name, is Trype, which I'm sad to say makes us Offal-Trypes. Embarrassing as that can sometimes be, it might not be *so* bad if we were chinless aristocrats, but we're not. Father's a butcher. The sign over his shop reads OFFAL-TRYPE, FAMILY BUTCHER (though no families are butchered on the premises).

The three of us live above the shop. It's not a big flat, but Mother makes it as nice as she can without the maid and housekeeper she says a woman of quality should have. So there you have me, in one big fat nutshell: Jerome Ignatius Granville Offal-Trype, butcher's son, living in a two-bedroom flat over the shop with my parents and a flushable toilet, 1906 anno domini. And that's the nutshell I would have stayed in if we hadn't visited the zoological gardens one November afternoon, but before I get to that I'd better mention a couple of other things. Such as that Father employed me (for a pittance) to deliver meat to customers who couldn't be bothered to carry it home themselves. I know I should have been grateful to have work because a lot of people didn't, but I couldn't bear the look, smell or feel of meat, any meat, any shape or form. I didn't even eat *cooked* meat if I could avoid it.

The worst of living above a butcher's shop was the stench of dead meat that seeped up through the floorboards. You didn't notice it most of the time you were indoors because you got used to it, but when you went home after being out for a while it really hit you. Hit me anyway, and Mother to some extent. I would groan as I climbed the stairs to the flat while she would pull a face and wave a hanky under her nose. She said the odour clung to her hair and clothes, and to cover it doused herself in a scent that was almost as bad. 'Mother,' I would say, 'that perfume is *killing* my nose nerves,' but she would tell me to put up with it because she wasn't going *anywhere* smelling of dead animals.

And so we come to the big day out that was to ruin my life. Mother made Father and me wear our best clothes for the occasion – he his Sunday suit, me my knickerbockers. We hate dressing up, Father and I, but there's only one boss in our house and it isn't us. Mother put on her best dress (blue), a big hat with feathers, gloves that went up to her elbows, and her fox fur stole, but stayed inside as long as possible while Father and I waited along the pavement for the tram. 'A lady cannot be seen loitering in the street,' she said in her most toffee-nosed voice.

There'd been thick swirly fogs for a week and today wasn't much better, so we were glad when the tram finally arrived. 'It's here, dear!' Father called, and Mother stepped off our step and walked like royalty towards the stop.

The Zoological Gardens and Menagerie had only been open a few days, but it looked like being a really popular attraction. I'd never seen so many people flocking to one place on any day of the week, and this was Sunday, the day most people stay at home and do nothing.

There were turnstiles at the entrance to the gardens. Some in the queue were grumbling about the price of entry. 'It'll never catch on if they keep charging this sort of money,' one man said loudly as he steered his family through. There were strange trees and shrubs all over the gardens, and enormous hot-houses stuffed with exotic plants, but what most people had come for was the menagerie (already being called the 'zoo' because it was easier). The menagerie/zoo was amazing. Cages and paddocks full of creatures no one had ever seen before in the flesh. Flamingos, for instance. Flamingos are really weird, all pink, with long curved beaks and legs like bent pencils. The lions and tigers were smaller than I'd expected from paintings and engravings, but the way they prowled about and eyed me through the bars fair took my breath away. And I loved the giraffes, gobbling leaves from the tops of trees, and the *Camelus bactrianus*, loping along with its two big hairy humps and snooty expression.

Entrance to almost all of the enclosures was forbidden, but there was one, *The Small Nocturnal Mammals House*, which visitors were permitted to go into. Mother was about to lead the way when Father mentioned that some of the nocturnal mammals would be bats.

'Bats?' Mother said. 'You mean *actual* bats?'

Father fluttered his fingers and hissed through his teeth. 'Yesss…'

She screwed her face up. 'Oh, I don't want to see things like *that*.'

'Thought you might not,' said Father.

'I've never seen a bat,' I said.

'I have,' he said. 'Dark night, it was. Came at me like it wanted to tear me head off.'

'And did it?'

'Yeah, this is a new one.'

I asked if I could go in and he said I could. So

while Mother went all shuddery at the thought of the bats, I strolled into *The Small Nocturnal Mammals House* alone. I didn't know it, but this was a mistake. A very big one...

Do you think you're funny?
Fancy yourself as a published author?

Send us a joke that would make Jiggy McCue laugh and it could feature in a Jiggy McCue book!

Email your joke to jiggyjokes@jiggymccue.com
or send it to us at Jiggy Jokes, Hachette Children's Books,
338 Euston Road, London NW1 3BH
Don't forget to include your name and age!

Here are some of our favourites so far...

Pupil: Would you tell me off if I didn't do anything, sir?
Teacher: No, of course not.
Pupil: Good. Cos I haven't done my homework!
Charlotte, age 10

Why does Jiggy keep losing his clothes?
Because he's underwear of what's happening!
Izabel, age 9

What do you call a chicken in a shell suit?
An egg!
Catie, age 10

There were two horses standing in a field.
One said to the other, 'I'm so hungry I could eat a horse.'
The other one said, 'Moo!'
Maddy, age 10

Why are football players never asked to dinner?
Because they're always dribbling!
Marta, age 11

www.jiggymccue.com
www.orchardbooks.co.uk